1492
New World Tales

Richard and Judy Dockrey Young

August House, Inc.
ATLANTA

Cover illustration and book design by Graham Anthony

Illustrations by Morgan Menter, pages 55, 59, 90, 98, 125, 139, 209, 219

Library of Congress Cataloging-in-Publication Data

Young, Richard, 1946-
  1492 : New World tales / Richard and Judy Dockrey Young.
      pages cm
  "Part of this collection was previously published under the title
Stories from the Days of Christopher Columbus, August House,
Little Rock, 1992."
   Summary: A collection of traditional tales, fables, and legends from
the cultures brought together or affected by the voyages of Columbus,
including those of Spain, Portugal, Italy, and the mainland and island
Indian tribes he encountered.
  ISBN 978-1-939160-73-7 (alk. paper)
  1. Tales. [1. Folklore.] I. Young, Judy Dockrey, 1949- II. Young,
Richard, 1946- Stories from the days of Christopher Columbus. III.
Title. IV. Title: Fourteen ninety-two. V. Title: New World tales.
  PZ8.1.Y857Aak 2013
  398.2--dc23
                            2013014101

With Gratitude to
Dr. Rolando Hinojosa-Smith
University of Texas at Austin
"The Dean of Mexican-American Letters"
who listened to Richard tell a medieval tale
in 1988 and inspired this medieval story collection.

Table of Contents

Preface: Kids' Life in 1492..8

Introduction: Setting Sail With Christopher Columbus...........11

STORIES:

On Board the *Pinta* 19
    • Don Juan Calderón

On Guanahaní...33
    • Cave of the Face Paint

On Board the *Niña* 41
    • The Cat Who Became a Monk
    • The Pig and the Mule
    • House Mouse and Country Mouse
    • Lady Owl's Child • King Lion and the Rabbit

In Zempoala 53
    • The Totonac • The Legend of Xanath
    • The Otomí
    • Old Dog and Young Coyote
    • The Aztec Letter • Little Rabbit and Coyote
    • The Aztec Overlords of Zempoala
    • Smoking Mountain • Hungry Coyote's Lament
    • Scary Aztec Stories • Wailing Woman
    • Skeleton's Revenge

In the Ruins of Tajín 96
    • The Dance of the Birds

On Board the *Santa María*...101
    • The Exile of El Cid • The Triumph of El Cid

On the Central American Mainland 118
    • The Dwarf of Uxmal

On the North American Mainland..123
    • The Mocama Band of the Timucua
    • The One-Legged Beings

On the South American Mainland...129
•	The Carib • Tamosi and the Tree of Life
•	Tamosi and the Big Canoe
On the Canary Islands...136
•	The Dark Sea • The Ghost Island
•	The Lady with the Candle • The Dragon's Blood Tree
•	The Fortunate Isles
On the Atlantic Shore of Portugal 146
•	The Iron Dancing Shoes • The Three Citrons of Love
•	The Tower of Ill Fortune
On the Atlantic Shore of Spain...........................172
•	Black and Yellow • Young Lovers from Teruel
•	Bastianito • The Witch of Amboto
On the Atlantic Shore of North Africa 206
•	Gold Coast African Stories
•	Why Anansi Has a Narrow Waist
•	Why Anansi Has a Bald Head
•	Moroccan Middle Eastern Funny Stories
•	Joha Bids on a Mule • Joha's Neighbor Asks a Favor
•	Joha's Mule Wanders Off • Joha's Son Drives a Nail
•	Joha and the Bucket Wheel • Joha and the Jack
•	Joha and the Joint of Meat
•	Moroccan Jewish Stories • The Golem of Ceuta
•	The Magic Pomegranate

Afterword for Teachers, Librarians and Parents....................229

Sources of These Stories.....................................237

Glossary of Words You May Not Know...............................245

Preface

Kids' Life in 1492

Historians divide the world's past into periods for collective study. The Middle Ages are considered to have begun in 1066 with the Norman Invasion of England, and end with the discovery of America on October 12, 1492. The age we live in now, which we rather pretentiously call the Modern Age, began October 13, 1492, and continues until today. This is a book of stories from that moment in history as the world left the Middle Ages and moved into the Modern Age.

In the year 1492, most of the people of Europe, North Africa, and North and South America relied on spoken words instead of written words. Very few people in those days knew how to read or write. Europe had many written languages, but the average man or woman, boy or girl, could not read the languages because there were not many opportunities for people to learn to read. Only a small number of schools existed, and since the printing press, invented by Johannes Gutenberg in 1440, was not yet in common use, large hand-copied books were too expensive for most people to afford.

On the American continents, the Aztec and Mayan Indians had written languages that used pictures instead of an alphabet. They even had hand-written books of folded bark paper. Most people could not read the pictograms, however, because only a small number of boys, chosen to be religious leaders when they grew up, were given the chance to learn the picture writing.

Without very many chances to go to school, most teenage men and women learned a trade by working as apprentices. They would help someone like a seamstress or blacksmith and learn the profession from a professional. Without knowing how to read and write, most young people learned all they knew by watching and listening. Instead of reading books or using an e-reader, they listened to stories told aloud. Instead of watching stories on television, at the movies, or on hand-held devices, everyone watched plays or listened to stories told out loud.

This book is a collection of stories that were being told in the year 1492 and have since been written down. Because five centuries have passed since 1492, these stories may not be written exactly the way they were told aloud, and these stories have all been translated into English instead of Spanish, Portuguese, Catalán, Taíno, Aztec, Maya, Carib, Totonac, Otomí, or any of the other languages they came from.

Each group of stories has a short introduction to help set the scene for where the story might have been told. Some stories sound so strange to us today that they are accompanied by an article called "The Story Behind the Story." (The first "Story Behind the Story" appears after the story itself. The others appear before the story they explain.) Read that if you want to understand the story better. After you have read these stories silently to yourself, you will enjoy reading or telling them aloud to others, just as they were told so long ago across the Atlantic Ocean from shore to shore in 1492.

Richard and Judy Dockrey Young
Reeds Spring, Missouri
October 12, 2013

Introduction

Setting Sail
with Christopher Columbus

More than five hundred years ago, on Friday, August 3, 1492, three small ships left the Spanish seaport of Palos de Moguer (pronounced PAH-lohss deh Mo-GAIR spelled out like English. The syllables in all capital letters are said louder than the rest.) The three ships sailed southwest to a chain of islands off the coast of Africa called the Canaries. The islands are known for their beautiful singing birds, which were named canaries after the islands. At the islands, the sailors made repairs on the three ships. They were not new ships, they were old "used" ships and had not been very well maintained. The sailors finished repairs and took on supplies for a longer voyage from the Canary Islands to the west.

The sailors were all from southern Spain, but some of the men's families had come to Spain from the Middle East, or from nearby Africa. These men and boys...there was a young cabin boy on each ship...sailed into unexplored and uncharted ocean on the most dangerous sea voyage anyone ever made up to that time.

Why would these men and boys...no women went along...go on such a dangerous journey? Their commander had a dream! He wanted to sail southwest from Spain and reach Cipangu (pronounced See-PAHNG-oo, which we call Japan today), China and India by a short sea route. The best globe-maker of the time,

Martin Behaim, had made a globe of the world that showed Japan right where Cuba really is. No one knew about the North and South American continents. The commander of the three ships sailed straight to that island…to Cuba, that is, not to Japan. Martin Behaim's globe was wrong.

The commander of this expedition was Christopher Columbus, to use his name the way we say it in English. Everyone who spoke Spanish called him Cristóbal Colón (pronounced Kreess-TOH-bahll Koh-LOHN.) People who spoke the Catalán language of the east coast of Spain called him Cristòfor Colom (Krees-TOH-fohr Coh-LOHM.) He had been given the title of Admiral of the Ocean Sea by King Ferdinand and Queen Isabella of Aragon and Castille, and all his men called him Admiral, or used his Spanish name. Columbus promised the King and Queen he would find the way across the wide, dangerous Atlantic Ocean to China and India and bring back the luxuries the small group of rich people in Europe wanted to buy.

Silk from China and cotton from India made softer and more comfortable clothes than what most Europeans wore. Tea from China and India was prepared by boiling water, which killed germs (back then no one knew that), and tasted better than the dirty water in the rivers and streams of Europe. Spices like cinnamon from the Orient made food taste better. The rich people in Europe were willing to pay a good price for these luxuries. Columbus and the King and Queen wanted to become rich by bringing goods from the Orient back to the countries of Europe.

The commander, the three ship's captains, and the sailors did not know – no one from Europe knew – that China was twice as far from Spain as Columbus had calculated, and that two huge continents, North America and South America, stood in his way. The prevailing winds blew the ships off course further south than the captains realized. The instruments they used to navigate were not as accurate as the ones used by sailors today.

After leaving the Canary Islands on September 6th, 1492, the three ships sailed west for about a month without so much as a glimpse of land. At the end of thirty days…it was then the first days of October…the sailors feared they had just enough food to last for the return trip to the Canaries, and they wanted to turn back. Columbus promised them that they would soon see land and offered a reward to the first sailor to see it. When the ships' crews went to sleep on the evening of October 11, 1492, they knew that if land was not seen in another day or two they would have to give up and return to the Canaries, then to Spain.

At two hours past midnight on the starry morning of Friday, October 12, 1492, the three small ships were sailing in a line, very much alone in uncharted waters three thousand miles west of the Canary Islands, the last land they had seen. On deck one sailor steered with the tiller, a long pole which turned the ship's rudder at the stern (back of the ship.) A second member of the crew stayed awake all night, quietly singing a song and saying a prayer as he turned the hourglass each hour to keep the time.

Just like today, men and boys in 1492 used nicknames. High in the forecastle (at the front of the ship nicknamed *The Pinta*) stood a man whose nickname was Rodrigo de Triana (Roh-DREE-go deh Tree-AH-nah.) His real, full name was Juan Rodríguez Bermejo, but there were nineteen other sailors named Juan and three others named Rodrigo on this voyage, so to tell him apart from others he was called by a nickname for his hometown of Triana. Looking ahead to the west, he spotted dark shapes on the horizon.

Rodrigo de Triana knew that the horizon on the open sea is always level, and that these dark shapes against the starry sky could be only one thing...land! The sailors had recently seen birds flying above and tree branches and other plant material floating in the water, two signs that land might be near. Rodrigo squinted hard into the night until he was sure of what he saw. Then he sang out the words that everyone had wanted for so long to hear:

"*Tierra! Tierra!*"..."Land! Land!"

The shouts alerted the watchman down on the main deck, who woke the Captain of the *Pinta*. The sailors quickly ran on deck and lowered all but one of the sails to make the ship slow down. The three ships, the *Pinta* (the "Painted One"), the *Niña* (the "Little Lady"), and the *Santa María* (the "Saint Mary") were sailing close in a line, and Captain Pinzón fired the canon of the *Pinta* alerting the other two ships. Their crews lowered their sails also. The ships began to jog back and forth, like people pacing back and forth, eagerly awaiting the dawn.

As the sun rose on October 12th, the sailors and the officers could see dark-skinned people on the shore of the small island. During this historic day, they would learn that the natives called the island Guanahaní (Gwah-nah-hah-NEE), and the chain of islands to which it belonged the Lucayas (Loo-CAH-yahs). [The name Guanahaní probably means Place of the Iguana, a kind of tropical lizard.] But for now the Spaniards knew only that the natives were dark-skinned like the people in the faraway land of India, one of the places Columbus had hoped to reach. Thinking this must be India, where the people have brown skin, Columbus incorrectly called this part of the sea the Indies, and called the people Indians.

He was wrong, of course, but the two names were used for hundreds of years, and are still used today.

Columbus, the captains of the other two ships, and several men equipped with swords and lances rowed ashore in a small boat called a launch. Columbus carried the royal flag of Spain and the two captains each carried an expedition flag, which had a green cross in the center and the letters F and Y on opposite sides of the cross, standing for Fernando and Isabel. Above each initial was a crown to show that these were the initials of the king and queen. Columbus claimed the island for Ferdinand and Isabel, even though he really had no right to do so. The land really should have continued to belong to the people who lived there.

On Guanahaní, Columbus and his men found beautiful ponds, and many strange trees, plants, and fruits they had never seen before. The native "Indians," who called themselves Lukku-cairi (LOO-koo-KAH-ee-ree or Lucayos, Taíno for "People of the Islands") came down to meet the launch. All day long Columbus' men and the Lukku-cairi visited. The Spanish managed to learn enough of the native language to talk a little with the Lukku-cairi, whom Columbus called Lucayos and who were part of the Taíno (Tah-EE-no) people, so most of the first meeting was trading and pointing and showing things to each other.

It was warm on the island, even in October, and the Taínos wore little or no clothing. The Spaniards laughed at the Indians for walking around almost naked, and the Indians laughed at the Spanish, who had on metal armor and heavy clothing even though they were obviously hot and sweating in that climate. The Indians had with them fish, fishing spears made of dried cane with a bone point, parrot feathers, and cotton thread to trade, but the Spanish wanted only one thing: the Indians' little nose ornaments, which were made of gold.

For the gold, the Spanish gave the Indians small bells, bright beads, pieces of colorful glass, and even pieces of broken pottery with designs in the ceramic. By European standards this was very unfair, gold was worth far more than those trinkets, but the Indians enjoyed the things the Spanish gave them in trade. The Lucayos believed the Spanish could get more gold by trading with the people of the islands we now call Hispaniola and Cuba. So, at least on that first day of the Modern Age, everyone was fairly happy with the meeting.

Columbus should have known something was wrong. His interpreter, Luís de Torres, tried to speak to the Lucayos in Arabic, a language spoken in parts of India. The "Indians" didn't understand a word. They were not "Indians," they were Native Americans. Columbus still called them "Indians" and insisted he had reached India. Of course, the real India was half a world farther west.

At the end of that fateful day when the people of Europe first came into permanent contact with the native people of the Americas, everyone returned to his own sleeping place.

The Lucayo Band of the Taíno Indians went back to their village of fifteen or so grass houses with high pointed roofs. A small fire was built in the firepit in the center of each hut, and the smoke went out the smokehole at the point of the roof. The Taínos settled down and told stories in their own language.

The sailors went back to their ships and as they prepared for sleep they passed the time, as always, by singing, gambling, and telling stories. Across the Atlantic, on the Canary Islands, in Spain, and in Portugal, where Columbus' family and the other men's families awaited them, people told stories that same night. On the east coast of Mexico (part of the mainland of North America), in the Totonac city of Zempoala, the Totonac, Otomí, and Aztec people also ended the day with romantic stories and scary storytelling. On the Yucatán Peninsula to the south, the Maya people told their tales. Farther away on the mainland of South America, the Carib people…for whom the Caribbean Sea is named…told their stories around cooking fires.

All these people, from different continents and cultures, spoke different languages, lived in different kinds of homes, wore different kinds of clothing, ate different kinds of food, and played different kinds of games, but they all had one thing in common: they all loved storytelling. Each region's stories were very different from each other, but as the world passed the first night of this Modern Age, this collection of stories is what they were probably telling.

18

Onboard the *Pinta*

Columbus' three ships sat at anchor as the sun was setting at about 6:00 p.m. on October 12, 1492. The man watching and turning the hourglass called it "the sixth hour after high noon." The sailors spent the evening as they always did, playing gambling games, singing, and telling stories from each sailor's home region. The ships rocked gently in the waves and the candle-lanterns swung as the sailors told their tales.

Each of Columbus's ships had a story of its own. Two of the ships were known by their nicknames instead of their real names. One was the *Pinta*, owned by Cristóbal Quintero. Sailors always gave ships girls' names, the nickname *Pinta* meaning "Painted Girl." Perhaps some of the ship's wooden parts were brightly painted. Perhaps "Painted Girl" meant a girl with make-up on going out on a date with a sailor. We do not know the official name of the *Pinta*. It has been forgotten in the five hundred years since she sailed.

It was from the *Pinta* that land had first been sighted that morning, giving the *Pinta* a very special place in world history.

Sailors stood at the rail, looking at the island in the starlight, thinking of home. The sailors felt proud and happy that they had been able to make such a dangerous and difficult trip and arrive safely. Perhaps a sailor told that night this very special, long, and funny adventure story from southern Spain about a legendary dangerous and difficult task:

Don Juan Calderón Kills Seven

Érase que era…Once it was that there was…in the last years
before the many small kingdoms that spoke Spanish and Catalán
were united under King Ferdinand and Queen Isabel, a little village
high in the Mountains of Moraine in the western part of what
would one day become Spain. In the village lived a short, chubby
leatherworker. His two-room house was made of whitewashed
stucco with a roof of red tile. The room in back was his living
quarters, with a fireplace and a table and a chair and a bed and a
great trunk at the foot of the bed where he kept his clothing. The
room in front was his shop, with his workbench and his tool chest
and a cabinet full of leather, and walls hung with saddles and
bridles and other leather goods for sale.

One fine morning he sat at his workbench, making a leather
belt for a rich, fat man who lived in the village. Just as he was
preparing to tool into the leather the designs that the rich man had
asked for, he sat back for a moment and began to think about what
he might have for his lunch.

He had only finished breakfast a few minutes before, but it was
never too early in the day for him to start thinking about lunch. His
name was Juan, this little leatherworker, and his family name was
Calderón, which means the same as "cooking pot." It was a good
name for a plump little man who thought about food a lot. He sat
back with his leather-headed hammer in his hand, and began to
daydream about his lunch.

"Let's see," thought Juan, "I could have some ham and some

bacon and some sausage and some bread and some olive oil and some..." While he was daydreaming, he grew very still. In fact, he did not move any at all. He sat so still that a little housefly, buzzing about above the workbench, forgot that there was a person down below.

The fly began to think that Juan was another piece of furniture. Flies have a very short memory. The fly flew down to the workbench and began to walk around until it found a little grain of sugar from the sweetbread Juan had eaten for breakfast. Then it called to its fly friends to come down and join it for a fly feast. Six more houseflies flew down and they all gathered, seven in a circle, around the grain of sugar, discussing fly politics or some such matter. Just at that moment, Juan ended his daydream.

"...and I could have some custard with caramel sauce for dessert."

Then Juan blinked his eyes and looked down for the first time in several minutes. There sat seven rude flies on Juan's workbench. How insulting! Using the only thing he had in his hand, his leather-headed hammer, Juan took the flies by surprise and killed all seven with one blow.

Squish!!!

Yucch! Fly guts. He brushed his workbench clean, and began to talk to himself as he sometimes did when there was no one to talk to.

"You know," he said to himself very proudly, "I imagine that no one else has ever killed seven houseflies with one blow before. I should do something to reward myself for such a great deed. I could use a new belt myself...for some reason my old one seems to be getting shorter! The rich man doesn't need this one I'm making until next week. I think I'll make this leather into a fine new belt for myself!"

He began to work with his hammer and tools, writing his name on his belt. J...u...a...n..., he wrote, C...a...l...d...e...r...ó...n. Since the leatherworker was a plump little man, he had a lot of belt left to write on, so he added the words "Kills Seven" in honor of the fact that he had killed seven flies with one blow of his hammer. He would have written "kills seven houseflies," but not even Juan was chubby enough for that many words on his belt! But there was still a little bit of room in front of his name, so he wrote the word Don which means "Very Important Mister," in front of his name.

He held up his new belt and read it out loud: "*Don Juan Calderón Mata Siete*." Very Important Mister Juan Calderón Kills Seven. He was very proud of his brave deed and of his new belt, and he decided to go out and show it off to his friends. He put on his brimless leather hat and swung his leather pouch of leatherworking tools over his shoulder. You see, when he went walking on the streets of his little town, people were always asking him to stop and fix a boot, or stitch up the loose threads on a bridle, or some other thing. Juan enjoyed the copper coins they paid him, and the chance to sit and visit while he worked. Last of all he put on his new belt, cinched it tight...only rich men had buckles on their belts...and set out to walk to the plaza to see his friends.

First he saw Don Diego, an old retired soldier of fortune, sitting on a bench by the street.

"Don Diego," Juan called out, "look at my new belt!" He turned to show off the writing on the back. Before he could explain about the houseflies, Don Diego read outloud, "Very Important Mister Juan Calderón Kills Seven..." and said, "Don Juan, I did not know that you had killed seven men in battle! I did not even know that you were a veteran!"

Don Juan tried to explain that it was only seven foolish houseflies that he had killed, but it was already too late. The truth crawls along the ground like a worm, but rumor has wings like a hawk. Don Diego was already calling out the news to his friends across the street.

By the time Don Juan had explained it all to Don Diego, seven other men had heard the rumor, and it was "Don Juan Calderón killed seven men in battle."

By the time the rumor reached the edge of the plaza, it had grown to "Don Juan Calderón killed seven men in battle with his bare hands."

By the time the rumor got to the front door of the cathedral, it had grown to "Don Juan Calderón killed seven men in battle with his bare hands, after the rest of the army had retreated in fear."

By the time the rumor got to the marketplace beyond the plaza, it had grown to "Don Juan Calderón killed seven men in battle with his bare hands, after the rest of the army had retreated in fear, in the great battle for the city of Valencia fighting alongside El Cid!"

No one stopped to remember that the Battle of Valencia had happened over two hundred years before and El Cid was buried for two centuries! No one questions a rumor!

A large crowd had gathered around Don Juan in the plaza, congratulating him as he tried to explain that it had only been seven foolish houseflies that he had killed. Just then, a knight in armor rode into the plaza on a great white horse. He dismounted, climbed the steps of the cathedral, and faced the crowd.

"Señores and señoras," he shouted, "a great tragedy has befallen Spain! The King of Granada has sent a giant to kill our King! We must have a champion who will fight this giant and save our King!"

All the people of the little town shouted at once, "Don Juan Calderón will do it! He killed seven..." Well, you know the rest!

And they all cheered, and they...well, ten of them picked up the little leatherworker, he was rather heavy, and carried him on their shoulders. They sat him on the knight's great war horse. The knight leaped astride the horse and they rode away to the great palace of the King!

Palace guards led Don Juan into the large hall where the King sat on his throne and greeted his guests. Don Juan bowed very low, and waited for the King to speak first.

"Greetings, Señor," said the king. "Could it be that you have come to prove yourself as my champion and save me from the giant?"

Don Juan bowed low again before he spoke. He wanted to explain that he was only a simple leatherworker, and he had killed only seven houseflies. He thought the best way to explain what he did for a living was to show off a sample of his work: his new belt he made for himself.

"Your Majesty," said Don Juan, "as you can see by this belt..." He turned around to show that he was a leatherworker, but the King read the inscription very quickly.

Before Don Juan could finish his sentence, the King said,"Very Important Mister Juan Calderón Kills Seven? Why, Señor, my personal bodyguard killed only five men when I led the soldiers in a war. You must be a great warrior. I name you my champion!" With that, he touched his shiny sword to Don Juan's shoulder as a sign of the little leatherworker's new rank.

Only moments later, it seemed, Don Juan marched out the city gates, with forty soldiers escorting him, headed for the grassy plain to meet the giant. "Well," thought the little leatherworker, "this is not so bad. Counting me there must be forty-two or three of us! I bet that old giant will be quaking in his boots with fear when he..."

But then the soldiers stopped and faced Don Juan, and raised their swords in a salute. Wishing him good luck, the escort went back through the city gates and slammed them shut.

Don Juan Calderón was all alone on the grassy plain by the River Guadalquivir (GWAH-dahl-kee-VEER.)

"Well," he said to himself, "this is not so bad. The giant may not come today. He may not even see little me here in the big, empty grassland."

Just then, over a nearby hill came the biggest giant Don Juan had ever seen, heard of, or imagined in his nightmares. The giant was as tall as seven men would be if they stood on one another's shoulders. The giant wore big black boots as high as a horse, and big, black, puffy pants as big as the sails of a ship. He carried a huge curved sword as long as three Spanish swords laid end-to-end! And he walked onto the grassy plain, right up to Don Juan, and bent down low to look at him.

"WHO ARE YOU?" asked the giant, in a voice like thunder.

The little leatherworker leaned back away from the giant's ugly head, and said, as bravely as he could, "Well, Your Enormousness, I am Juan Calderón... and the King..." he tried to gather his courage "has sent me ...has sent me.."

"YES?" roared the giant.

"...has sent me to make you a new belt!" It was all Don Juan could think of to say.

The giant stood upright again. "GOOD!" he boomed."SHOW ME A SAMPLE OF YOUR WORK."

"Well," thought Don Juan to himself, "this is not so bad. I will show him this belt, and he will read what it says, and he will think I am a great warrior. He'll probably be shaking in his big black boots when he reads this!" So he turned and bowed down so the giant could read the writing on the belt. The giant stooped very low...well, low for a giant...and looked very closely at the belt, with eyeballs as big as melons.

"Well, Your Giganticness," said the little leatherworker, "What do you think of the inscription?"

"I'M FROM GIBRALTAR (Hee-brahll-TAHR)," thundered the giant, "I CAN'T READ SPANISH!"

Oh, the poor little leatherworker! Here was the only person in the whole wide world he would like to have fooled with the belt, and the giant couldn't read what it said! Don Juan began to think very fast.

"HOW MANY COWSKINS WILL WE NEED FOR THE BELT?" boomed the giant, eager to receive his gift from, he presumed, the King.

Well, now, this was something Don Juan was good at! Making things from leather! He looked up at the giant's waist, and thought about it for a moment.

"Seven," he called up to the giant. "We will need seven cowskins."

"I'LL BE RIGHT BACK," said the giant, in a voice like

28

waves crashing on the rocks in a storm. And he turned and stomped away, stepping over the mountains as he went.

When he was gone, Don Juan said to himself, "Well, this is not so bad! Now that he's gone, I can run away and... and..." then he knew he could not run "...and I would be a coward, and the people of my village would be so disappointed in me."

So he sat down and waited. He did not have long to wait. Over the mountains came the giant, with three dead cows under one arm and four dead cows under the other.

The giant threw down the cows, and skinned them with his huge curved sword. He dragged the skins over to the little leatherworker, and boomed, "GET TO WORK!"

Don Juan got to work.

He opened his pouch of tools and took out his knives, cut each skin into a rectangle, and laid them end-to-end in the grass. He slit the leftover skin into long strips, and used a sharp awl to punch holes along the edges of the leather rectangles. Using the strips of skin like thread, he began to stitch the skins together into a huge belt thirty feet long.

"Well," thought Don Juan to himself, "this is not so bad. When he gets this belt on, I'll bet that old giant will be so grateful that he will want to be my friend." So he looked up at the giant and asked in a loud voice, "Oh, excuse me, Your Hugeness, but what shall we do after I finish your nice new belt?"

The giant folded his arms and looked down at Don Juan. "AFTER YOU FINISH THE BELT, I WILL SQUASH YOU WITH MY THUMB!"

Now, if Don Juan were to name all the things he liked to do, being squashed by the thumb of a giant would have been very near the end of the list. Once again, he began to think very fast.

"Well, Your Extremely Bigness, it's an awfully hot afternoon. Couldn't we have something to drink?"

"GOOD IDEA! I'LL BE RIGHT BACK," thundered the giant, and he stomped away over the hill. Don Juan quickly finished lacing the pieces together, completing the huge belt. He grabbed one end and slowly dragged the belt down to the River Guadalquivir, and pushed the enormous belt into the water. He let it soak for a few minutes, then slowly pulled the long, wet, heavy leather strip back out onto the grass.

Just then, the giant came tramping back over the hill, carrying three barrels of wine under one arm, and four barrels of wine under the other. He dropped the barrels beside the little leatherworker, and used his giant sword to cut the tops off all seven barrels. The giant lifted a barrel, and drank from it as if it were a cup. Don Juan took off his brimless leather hat and dipped it into one of the barrels and used it as a cup.

While the two were quenching their thirst in the hot, bright afternoon sun, Don Juan suggested, "Why don't you try on your new belt, Your Great Bigness?"

"GOOD IDEA!" the giant bellowed. He stood up, picked up the huge belt, and wrapped it around his waist.

"Cinch it good and tight," Don Juan shouted up to the giant who towered over him. The giant wrapped the leather over itself and cinched the belt very tight.

"IT'S WET!" boomed the giant suspiciously.

"Oh, Your Immenseness," said Don Juan, "it was a little bloody, so I washed it off. Let's finish our drink."

The giant sat back down and continued drinking wine in the hot afternoon sun. Pretty soon he began to yawn and blink. After six barrels of wine, he forgot all about the little leatherworker, and laid down on the grassy plain to take a nap. Don Juan moved over to sit in the shade of the sleeping giant and finish his hatful of wine. The giant began to snore.

Don Juan wiped sweat off his forehead and put his hat on. He stood up and stepped back to survey his work. It was a beautiful belt, with the spotted cow hair to the outside. But it was an ugly giant snoring in the hot sun of afternoon. Slowly the hot sun dried the fresh, wet leather, and it began to shrink. The belt grew tighter and tighter as the leather shrank tighter and tighter…

…until it crushed the giant to death!

Don Juan picked up his pouch of tools and walked calmly back to the city gates.

Don Juan was a hero! The entire city came out to see him made a knight of the realm. The King gave him forty pieces of gold as warrior's pension, and a beautiful red sash that said "Friend of the King" on it. Caballero (Cah-bahl-YEH-roh) Juan (for so knights were called) was given a white horse to ride home on.

A big white horse.

In his home village up in the foothills he was greeted by a cheering crowd of his friends. Twenty of them picked him up on their shoulders – he was heavier than ever, carrying his bag of gold – and carried him to the plaza, where they sang and danced and ate fine foods and had the biggest feast day the town had ever seen. As the sun was coming up the next day, everyone said, "*Buena Madrugada!*" (BWEH-nah mahd-throo-GAH-dthah) "Good dawning to you," and went home.

Caballero Juan Calderón went to his little house that he had left early that morning. He hung his red sash in the cabinet in his shop, and went into his bedroom. He took off the belt that had brought him so much trouble, rolled it up, and put it in the trunk at the foot of his bed.

And he never, ever, wore that belt again.

On Guanahaní

The sun had been down half an hour on October 12, 1492, and it was about 6:30 p.m. by modern standards of timekeeping. On Guanahaní, in a round grass hut with a high roof, a family of Lucayos (Loo-KAH-yohss)...a band of the Taíno (Tah-EE-noh) people...sat around the firepit, or swung in their hammocks. They ate pineapple, pieces of a white bread made of manioc, fish they had caught on their reed spears, and sweet potatoes. Other nights they might eat squash, and beans, with shellfish or turtle from the shallow tidal lagoons. Sometimes they ate crab meat and corn on the cob, just as we enjoy in the United States.

Almost everyone in the house painted their faces and bodies with black stripes of the acidic juice of the jagua plant, and red paint made from the annatto tree. The language they used telling their stories would sound strange to us today, but we would recognize some of the words they spoke because even today we use the Taíno words (shown here in English) hammock, maize, potato, barbecue, maraca and canoe. We can see part of the Taíno way of life in these words: they went fishing in canoes (canoa), they dried and barbecued fish on a wooden frame (barabicu), and after eating potatoes (batata) and maize (mahiz) [corn], they might sing and dance to the music of the maraca (maraca) a kind of rattle made from a gourd, and finally go to sleep in their hammock (hamaca).

This Taíno story is so strange that you may need to read the Story Behind the Story first. It appears after the story, and explains many odd things in The Cave of the Face Paint.

The children were swinging in their hammocks as an older woman told the oldest Taíno story in the gathering darkness. It is a story of creation of the Taíno People.

The Cave of the Face Paint

In the Beginning of Time, on the nearby Great Island, there was a place called Caonao (Kow-NOW). In that place there is still today a mountain named Cauta (KAH-oo-tah). In the mountain are two caves.

One is called Cave of the Face Paint. Inside the cave there was no light. All was black like the black face and body paint we make from the juice of the jagua (HAH-gwah) fruit, and for that plant the cave was named. It is from that cave that we Taíno People have come. The other cave is called the Cave of No Importance. It is from that cave that all the lesser people of the earth have come.

In the Cave of the Jagua Paint, we Taíno People lived in complete darkness. We never went out into the Sun, and were afraid of its light. We believed that if we went into the bright sunlight, the Sun had the power to change us into other creatures. We put a guard at the mouth of our cave to keep strangers away and keep Our People from wandering out into the terrible light during the day. This guard was named He-Who-Does-Not-Blink.

He-Who-Does-Not-Blink did a poor job of guarding the cave-mouth. He went out one night, when it was dark and safe, and did not return to the cave before dawn, as he was supposed to. The Sun caught him and turned him into a lizard. Since the lizard couldn't speak to stop them, some people went out in the bright sunlight to fish in the sea. The Sun caught them and turned them into cherry-plum trees.

One man named Guajayona (Gwah-hah-YOH-nah), who lived in our cave, was called Proud One because of his courage. People listened to him and obeyed him. Proud One sent Yahubaba, (Yah-hoo-BAH-bah) called the Old One, to gather some soap plant so the people could bathe in the stream inside the cave. Old One and a few other men went out by night, but he and the men moved too slowly coming back. The Sun rose. The Sun caught them and turned them into the song birds that sings in the morning, the way the nightingale sings at night.

Proud One said we should be brave and leave our cave and go out into the sunlight. He painted his face with the black paint made from the juice of the jagua fruit to protect him. He called for everyone to follow him. We women followed. We planned to come back with good things to eat and wear. The men were afraid and stayed behind. The men kept the children with them. The children cried at the cave-mouth when their mothers went out, and the Sun turned the children into the little frogs who sing at night and are now happy to be outside.

We women walked in a line behind Proud One, out into the sunshine, and became the grandmothers of all Our People. We live in the sunlight and we are happy.

The Story Behind the Story:

Lucayos is the name the people called themselves while living in the Caribbean Sea on the island Guanahaní. The name comes from the Taíno Indian words Lukku-Cairi meaning "island people." Their word for island, cairi became the Spanish word cayo and the English word cay meaning a very small island. Taíno is the name of the combined tribe of American Indians that made their homes on the northern islands in the Caribbean Sea. Guanahaní is the name the people gave to their small island now known as Samana Cay. Modern research proves that Samana Cay was the first place Columbus landed in the New World. Samana Cay is uninhabited today, but archaeologists have found artifacts on the island that prove it was inhabited by Lucayos in 1492. In the Beginning of Time, the Taíno believe, this story explains where the people came from. It is told in many versions on different islands. This is how it might have been told on Samana Cay on the night of October 12, 1492. The Great Island is the large island south of Samana Cay, known today as Hispaniola. Two nations occupy that island today: Haití and the Dominican Republic. Caonao means "the Place of Gold," a well-known region of the Dominican Republic. Cauta was the name the Taíno gave the mountain from which they emerged. There are many mountains in the Dominican Republic but we don't know today which one was called Cauta in 1492. The Taíno people called their cave Caciba-jagua (Kah-SEE-bah-HHAH-gwah) or Cave of the Jagua Plant (HHAH-gwah.) Cave of the Face Paint is another way to say the same thing. The jagua plant is a small tropical tree with a fruit that has lots of seeds but can be eaten. The juice of the jagua fruit is acidic like fresh-squeezed lemon juice, and if painted on the skin it makes a mild burn mark like a blue-black tattoo. The "tattoo" lasts about three weeks before the skin heals and the mark disappears. The other cave on Cauta Mountain was called by the long name Amayaúna (Ah-MA-EE-yah-OO-nah), meaning Cave of No Importance. The Taíno didn't think anyone else on earth was smart but themselves, an idea that many people had in ancient times. The guard at the cave was named Mácocael (MAH-koh-kah-ell), which probably means He-Who-Does-Not-Blink. Some people who tell this story say the Sun turned him into the lizard, others say he was turned into stone. The Taíno people believed in those days that the Sun was a powerful being. Scientists today point out that all energy… wood, coal, oil, gas, water, electrical, atomic and solar power…all come from the sun. The Taíno were right in part of their belief. The sun is very powerful! The Sun changed some people into cherry-plum trees. Scientists call these trees myrobalan or by the scientific name spondias lutea. The people in Taíno stories all have long names in a language most people don't know, so we give them names we can say easily. There are many plants whose roots or sap can be used as soap. We don't know today which plant the Taínos used in 1492. You can hear in this story how the Taíno people in those days explained that the Sun had made all the animals and plants out of people, and how the Taíno people came out into the world to live in the sunlight.

On Board the *Niña*

Another of Columbus's ships was the called the *Niña*, and sailors saying this nickname would have thought of "The Little Lady." The nickname probably comes from the fact that the ship was owned by a family with the last name Niño, meaning Junior. The true name of the *Niña* was Santa Clara. The *Niña* was so small that she could float in a modern swimming pool, yet she and her sister ships traveled thousands of miles across open sea, through storms and other dangers, to come to this New World.

Juan Arias was the teenage cabin boy on the *Niña*. He had heard stories called *exemplos* (eh-SHEHM-plohss, or examples; fables with a moral) all his young life. Most of them were funny, like old-fashioned jokes, so they were told over and over again.

Perhaps the cabin boy told one of these stories, and other sailors told others, as he turned the hourglass at about 7:00 p.m. on October 12, 1492.

The Cat Who Became a Monk

This is the story of the cat who turned himself into a monk. In one of the monasteries of Spain, in the dining hall, there lived a cat who had killed and eaten all the mice except one large mouse which had always escaped him.

One day, the cat thought of a way to catch the mouse. He went to the room where one of the monks lived and got a pair of scissors. He cut a bald patch on the top of his head, which was how the monks wore their hair.

Next, he went to the room where one of the monks was washing the laundry. Without asking, he borrowed the smallest monk's robe, that a boy wore, and put it on.

The cat pretended to be a monk. He walked along on his hind legs like a monk and went to prayers with the other monks. At dinnertime, the cat walked in and sat on a bench at the table, just like the other monks.

When the big mouse saw this, he thought, "The cat has become a monk! He will only eat the food prepared for him in the kitchen, like the other monks do. He won't eat me now."

Out came the mouse from his mouse house. He danced along the floor under the monks' table, eating the scraps they dropped by accident. Finally the mouse came right under the feet of the cat.

The cat jumped down and caught the mouse.

"Wait!" said the fat mouse. "You can't eat me! You're a monk!"

"Clothing doesn't change who I am," said the cat. With that, he ate the mouse.

Clothes do not make a cat into a monk.

And let that be a lesson to us all!

The Pig and the Mule

Two animals lived on the farmstead of a good man of Spain. The mule worked hard in the fields, side by side with the man, and each evening he was given oats to eat. The pig did no work at all, but just slept and grunted and pushed his nose in the ground sniffing for things to eat. Yet every evening the pig was given all the stale bread and table scraps from the household.

"That pig has an easy life," the mule thought to himself. "He does no work and yet he eats as well as a person. I think I will pretend to be ill, and get myself some special food, too."

The mule lay down as if he were ill. The farmer found him and said, "The mule has fallen ill. We must feed him to make him well."

And feed him they did, with fresh bread and water, ground meal from the kitchen, and green vegetable tops from the garden.

At first the mule ate only a little, as if he were really ill. Then, as days went by, he ate more and more and began to grow fat.

Soon winter was coming, and the farmer sent for the butcher to come from the village. The mule watched in horror as the butcher, with an axe and a knife, killed the fattened pig and cut him up for meat.

The mule feared that the farmer would have him butchered next! And he thought to himself, "I would rather work hard in the fields for the rest of my life than be fattened up this fine summer only to be hung up as meat in the pantry in autumn."

With that the mule, pretending to be well from his illness, ran out of the stable and into the yard where the farmer stood. The mule began to dance about, and sang, "Hee haw! Hee haw!"

The farmer was delighted to see his old mule well again, and the two went right to work. The mule worked hard all his life and never complained again.

And let that be a lesson to us all!

House Mouse and Field Mouse

There were two mice who were cousins, but one lived in the farmhouse and the other lived in the countryside.

It happened that they met in the yard one day, and the house mouse said, "Greetings, Cousin. Tell me what it is you eat in the fields every day."

"Wild beans," answered the field mouse, "and wheat and dried barley grains."

"Well," said the house mouse, "those are rather slim rations. I am much surprised that you don't waste away from hunger."

"Tell me, Cousin," said the field mouse, "what is it you dine on?"

"Well," said the house mouse, "I eat bread and cheese and fine meat and things that fall from the people's table. You should join me for supper some evening and we'll dine on the best!"

This pleased the field mouse very much and he agreed to come to the house that very evening. As the sun went down, the field mouse and the house mouse came out of the mouse hole and into the kitchen where the family sat at the table. They scampered about and ate things that fell to the floor.

Just about that time, along came the fat old cat that lived in the house, and she pounced on the field mouse and almost ate him! He wiggled away and ran for the mouse hole, with his house cousin close behind him.

"What was that?" asked the field mouse.

"Just the cat," said the house mouse. "You get used to her. You should dine with me more often. It would be great fun."

"But doesn't the cat ever catch mice?" gasped the field mouse.

"Oh," said the house mouse, "she ate my father and she ate my mother and has almost eaten me a few times."

"No, thank you," said the field mouse. "I would not wish to gain the whole Mouse World if the danger were that great. I'll stay in the field and eat my grains and beans, and leave you to your fine food and your dinner guest."

As the field mouse went out of the house he said to himself, "I'd rather gnaw on a bean than have fear gnawing on me!"

And let that be a lesson to us all!

Lady Owl's Child

It happened that all the animals called a council among themselves and asked that every kind of animal send a representative to the Court of the Animals. Now, it was a great honor to be selected to go to the Court of the Animals, and Lady Owl was very proud when the night birds selected her son to go as their representative.

The owl's son set out by night, of course and flew toward the great clearing in the forest where the court was to be held. Only after the son was gone did his mother discover that he had left without putting on his fine new shoes that he had wanted to wear at court.

Lady Owl tried to think of which animal was the fastest so she could send the shoes by way of that animal to get to court as soon as her son arrived. Then he could put on his new shoes. Lady Owl decided that the rabbit was fastest. She called at the home in the ground of Lady Rabbit and asked her if she were going to court.

"Yes, I am," Lady Rabbit replied.

"My son forgot his shoes," said Lady Owl. "Would you take them to him?"

"Of course," replied Lady Rabbit. "How will I know which one is your son?"

Lady Owl answered, "Oh, my son will be the most handsome bird there."

"Then," said Lady Rabbit, "your son must be the dove with beautiful white feathers."

"Oh, no," said Lady Owl.

"Then he must be the peacock with long feathers of many colors in his tail!" exclaimed Lady Rabbit.

"Oh, no," said Lady Owl. "He is neither of those birds. Why, the dove is all dark meat, and the peacock has such ugly feet!"

"I'm sorry," said Lady Rabbit. "You'll have to describe your son to me so I'll know which one he is."

"Well," said Lady Owl, "my son has a head just like mine and feathers just like these and feet just like these." She tilted her head, and showed her own wings and feet to Lady Rabbit. "And he'll be the handsomest bird there, and that's who you give the new shoes to."

Lady Rabbit smiled and took the shoes and hopped all the way to the Court of the Animals. She gave the shoes to the owl who was very grateful. Later, Lady Rabbit was talking to King Lion and she told him how Lady Owl had described her son.

"Yes," said old King Lion thoughtfully, "if you're in love with a frog, you think that frog is the moon. If you're in love with a toad, she looks like a queen to you. If you are a mother, you think your son is the most handsome son in the world."

And let that be a lesson to us all!

Greedy King Lion and the Rabbit

Once there was a fierce lion in a faraway land. In this land there was plenty of water and grassland, and many beasts lived there. But these beasts were cruel to one another because of their fear of the lion, who ate one of the beasts each day.

One day the beasts all came together in a council and discussed the lion problem. They talked most of the night, while the lion slept, and by the next morning they had reached an agreement. They sent representatives of each animal to meet with the lion before he became hungry for his midday meal.

"Great King Lion," said the beasts, "every time you take one of us it is a great insult and a great affront to us, and we live in fear of you. We have held a council, and we have an offer to make to you.

"If you will leave us alone to eat and drink and go about the grassland in peace each day, then we promise to select one from among us each day, and send him to you at midday as tribute."

This pleased King Lion, for it meant he would not have to hunt for his midday meals anymore. He agreed.

This went well for a while, with each kind of animal selecting one of its members to go to the lion as a tribute to be eaten by him, and to keep peace in the land.

One day the rabbits were to send a rabbit as tribute. They drew lots among them, and it fell to a smart, young rabbit to go and be eaten by the lion. The young rabbit was not very happy with the arrangement; he did not especially wish to become a lion's lunch.

"If I may speak a moment before I go," said the rabbit to the Council of the Animals, "I will tell you of a plan that will do you no harm, and in fact will end up doing you good. My plan will allow you all to escape from the tyranny of the lion and it will allow me to escape becoming his lunch."

"What must we do?" the rabbits and all the other animals asked.

"Whoever takes me to the lion," said the rabbit, "must take me very slowly. Let them take so long that by the time we arrive, it will be past the lion's lunchtime. I will do the rest."

"That pleases us," said the animals, and they agreed.

As the sun reached the high point in the sky, the lion grew hungry and angry as his tribute was not on time. He stood up and looked to his right and to his left: no tribute in sight. Soon he began to pace angrily back and forth. At last, here came the rabbit, hopping very slowly along, and without a procession of animals to escort him to the lion.

"Where is the tribute procession of animals?" demanded the lion. "And why are you so late in arriving? Why have the beasts broken their agreement with me?"

"I am the tribute of the beasts," said the young rabbit, "and I bring you a rabbit for your midday meal...myself. I am sorry to be so late, but that other lion saw the tribute procession and told the animals, 'You should give that rabbit to me instead of to the lion you're going to see.'"

"Other...lion?" asked the lion suspiciously. Male lions don't like other male lions!

"But I said to him," the rabbit went on, "No, this rabbit...me... is for the king of the beasts, the lion who is our master, and this rabbit is for his midday meal. You had better not take this rabbit and eat him yourself or the lion, our master, will be very angry."

"What other lion?" growled the lion, getting angry.

"But that other lion wouldn't let it go at that," the rabbit continued. "He said, 'Tell that lion, the king of beasts, that I want to fight him.' And with that, he took another of the rabbits from the tribute procession. I came here after all the other beasts had run away. I wanted to come and complain to you about it."

"Go with me," snarled the lion, "and show me where this other lion is."

"Let me ride your back," said the rabbit. "I'll show you where to go."

The lion let the rabbit ride on his back and off they went to a deep, clear pool of water that the rabbit directed the lion to.

"He's down in that pool," said the rabbit. "You'd better be careful. He can probably beat you! He's pretty mean!"

The lion crept to the edge of the deep pool and looked in, and saw his own reflection in the water. It was a lion, with an angry look on his face, and a rabbit on his back!

The king of beasts put the rabbit down and dove into the pool to kill the other lion, not doubting for a moment that there was another lion at the bottom of the pool. Diving deeper and deeper in search of the lion, the king of the beasts was drowned.

And the young rabbit went back to the council of the beasts and told them that the lion was dead, and they had secured their freedom.

And let that be a lesson to us all!

On the Mainland of Mexico

By a strange mathematical coincidence, about 1,492 miles west of where Columbus's ships lay offshore on the night of October 12, 1492, several great American Indian civilizations inhabited the southern end of the North American continent in what we now call México.

In Zempoala

On the coast of the Gulf of Mexico...that leads into the Atlantic Ocean...there was a great city called Zempoala (Sehm-poh-AH-lah. Located near the modern Mexican city of Veracruz.) Because the mainland is farther west than the Island of Gunanahaní it was still about 7:00 p.m. on October 12, 1492, in Zempoala, by our modern standards, when the sailors on the *Niña* finished telling stories.

Three different groups of Indian people lived in Zempoala: Totonacs (TOH-toh-nahks), Otomies (Oh-toh-MEEZ), and a few Aztecs who were foreign overlords. Like any great city, some of the people of Zempoala were rich and others were poor and hard-working. Like the kingdoms that fought each other four hundred years earlier in El Cid's lifetime in Spain, the Indian people of the mainland of Mexico often fought each other. Columbus never met these tribes of Mexican Indians, but after nightfall, each of the three tribes told stories in their homes in the city of Zempoala. The following stories come from all three tribes living in Zempoala: Totonacs, Otomies, and Aztecs.

The Totonacs

Most of the people in Zempoala were members of the Totonac nation. They called themselves Tutunaku (TOO-too-NAH-koo) and they called their language by the long name Tutunakutachawin (Too-too-NAH-koo-tah-CHAH-ween.) They built large cities with palaces and temples and constructed huge pyramids of stone over great mounds of dirt. The Totonacs lived as an independent kingdom until the year we call 1480, when they were conquered by the Aztecs who lived farther west (where Mexico City stands today.) The Totonac Indians liked to tell stories about the past glory days of the Totonac Empire, and its most famous city Tajín, during the years we call A. D. 600-1200. Here is such a story. [The linnet in the legend is the bird scientists call Carpodacus mexicanus.]

The Legend of Xanath

In the great Totonac city of Tajín, a family of nobles lived in a small stone house near the Great Pyramid of the Niches. The oldest daughter in this family was named Xanath (Shah-NAHT-hh), and she was the most beautiful young woman in Tajín. She was very religious, and went every day to the temple of Chac Mool (Chahk-MOHL), the rain god, to leave an offering on the plate the reclining statue held upon its stomach.

One day, on the way to the statue of Chac Mool, she heard someone whistling. It was so beautiful that she turned from her errand and followed the sound of the music. She found a handsome young man sitting on a rock at the edge of the Ceremonial Grounds. She sat down and listened to him whistle. His songs often included the whistling call of the beautiful bird called a linnet.

When he finished the song, the two introduced themselves. His name was Tzarahuín (TSAH-rah-WEEN), which means linnet! The two spent an hour sitting and talking, singing and laughing. Xanath completely forgot her errand to the Chac-Mool shrine.

Xanath was a noblewoman and Tzarahuín was only a food vendor. Her family did nothing for a living; they were wealthy. His family were farmers. Tzarahuín was well known among the royal family because he had often whistled songs for the members of the royal household when he delivered anonas, pineapples and edible gourds to the back door of the palace. Despite the differences in their families, the two fell deeply in love. They met as often as they could, when she was on her way to the Temple of Chac Mool and he was on his way to the market to sell his crops

One day, as Xanath was waiting at the Temple of the Niches for Tzarahuín to walk past carrying vegetables on a tumpline, one of the stone images of Totonac gods came to life and came crawling out of his niche. He was the Fat God of Joy, who loved to eat, play games and have parties. He grew from his size as a small, carved stone statue into his life size self with a bulky belly, shaved forehead and triple feather headdress. Every ancient god could be recognized by their physical attributes when they took on human form. The Fat God of Joy loved having beautiful women around him, and Xanath was the loveliest girl he could ever remember seeing.

He used magic in his eyes to see her everywhere she went that day, and at last he approached her to speak with her. Xanath saw that he was a god…they look different from mortal men…and ran from him in fear. Again he appeared before her and asked to speak to her. Again she ran away. On his third appearance before her, Xanath waited and listened to what the fat god had to say.

The Fat God asked Xanath to become one of his many brides, but she said she was in love with a mortal man and could not accept. Unaccustomed to being turned down, the Fat God went to Xanath's father and by magic made him even wealthier. Then he asked for Xanath's hand in marriage and her father, overjoyed at his new wealth, agreed.

Xanath's noble father ordered her to wed the Fat God. Xanath refused. The angry Fat God turned cruel and forced the King of Tajín to execute Xanath. When she was buried, Tzarahuín came and whistled at her grave. Then he committed suicide and was buried beside her. Out of Xanath's grave grew a delicate plant with white flowers and the most beautiful smell of any flower on the earth.

From a hole in the ground at Tzarahuín's grave flew tiny stingless bees. The bees and the flowers are in love, and from their courting in the gardens and jungles comes the most delicious plant product of all…vanilla.

The Fat God of Joy is forgotten. No one remembers his name. But everyone on this earth knows and treasures the sweetness of the vanilla bean and remembers the love of Xanath and Tzarahuín.

The Otomís

Several hundred inhabitants of the city of Zempoala were members of a tribe known to the Aztecs as Totomítl (Toh-toh-MEETL) meaning archer, as in "archers who hunt birds with bows and arrows." In Spanish they are called otomíes (Oh-toh-MEE-ehs.) In English we say Otomís (Oh-toh-MEEZ.) These people probably came down from a highland valley north of where Mexico City stands today. They were craftsmen and traders, and may have been brought to Zempoala by force by the Aztecs. Otomís from the Mezquital Valley...who were probably the ones in Zempoala...call themselves by the almost-impossible-to-pronounce name Hñähñuh. If you would like to learn to say it, just for fun, start by clearly pronouncing the English "h" [like in hat or hot], then the Spanish "ñ" [like the –ny- in canyon or barnyard]; then say the sound "ä", that in Otomí is pronounced halfway between "ah" as in father and "oh" as in open; then clearly pronounce "h" again, then another Spanish "ñ" , followed by the vowel "uh", just like when you ask someone "Uh...What did you say?" It sounds funny to us...but then, English sounds funny to Otomís!

Old Dog and Young Coyote

A family of Otomís lived in a house made by planting tall, straight cactus in a square pattern, and, when the catus grew tall, adding a roof of mesquite branches and wide leaves. Their cook fire was outdoors, and the one or two days a year that it rained, they ate cold food inside. Their home was in the high desert valley north of the Aztec capital city of Tenochtitlán (Teh-NOHTCH-tee-TLAHN.) The valley is known today as the Mezquital (MEHS-kee-TAHL.) One day it rained. The family sat inside their cactus house. The father told this story about a tsatyó (tsah-tee-OH [pronounce the ts just like English ts in cats] Otomí for dog), one of several species of Indian dogs found in America before 1492.

Old Dog was sitting in the pale shade of a mesquite bush, looking sad. A young coyote came along and looked at him.

"What are you?" asked the coyote.

"I'm a dog, same as you," said the old dog.

"You smell wrong," said Young Coyote. "You smell like wood smoke and Hñuh (HHnyUH: people)."

"The Hñuh are good to me. They feed me. I protect their cactus den. I keep snakes and skunks away."

"Why are you sad?"

"I heard my master talking inside the cactus den. He said I was too old to do any good. He said he was going to run me off. I don't want to go."

"I have a plan," said Young Coyote. He bent down and whispered in Old Dog's ear.

The following morning, Woman came out. Old Dog didn't know names. Woman had Baby with her. She sat Baby down and gave him some sweet cactus fruit to chew on. Baby chewed and cooed. Woman went back into the cactus den to get something.

Young Coyote ran out from behind a big tuxwadá (Toosh-wah-DAH: a cactus called *maguey blanco* in Spanish.) He gently grabbed Baby's foot in his teeth and began to growl and slowly drag Baby along the dust. He was very careful not to hurt Baby. Baby laughed.

Woman came out of the house screaming! Man came rushing out with his obsidian-bladed stalk knife!

Old Dog raced around from behind the cactus den, barking and jumping around.

Young Coyote let go of Baby and ran away yelping in fear. Old Dog ran a few steps after the coyote...that was all he could run... and barked and barked at the fleeing thief.

Woman picked up Baby, who was giggling. Woman hit Man with the flat of her paw. Old Dog didn't know hands.

"You will not run Old Dog off!" said Woman, angrily. "See how well he guards the cactus den! He will live here all his days!"

That night Woman gave Old Dog a bone with rabbit meat on it. Old Dog waited until she went back in the cactus den. Young Coyote came sneaking out from behind the tuxwadá and he and Old Dog ate the meat and gnawed the bone, just as dogs always do.

The Aztec Letter

Otomí traders walked along many dusty roads, taking items to and from the large Aztec cities to the small Otomí villages. One day a trader was walking a path and came to an Otomí hut just at midday mealtime.The traveler stood outside and called out loudly.The woman came to the door and answered him.

"I will pay you for a meal," he said.

"Come in," she said. "My man is away at the Aztec city of Tenochtitlán, and he has sent me a bark paper with pictograms. I cannot read them. I will make you tortillas and rabbit stew if you will read to me the paper."

The traveler agreed, and she made the meal, which they ate together.

After the meal she gave him the bark paper, and he turned it this way and that, looking at it.

"Sad news. Such sad news," he said shaking his head. "Such sad news for you."

"What is the sad news," asked the woman, very worried.

"The sad news is that…neither one of us can read!"

Little Rabbit and Coyote

A little rabbit was sitting in a rare clump of grass, waiting for his mother to return. A coyote came up after dark and sniffed at the grass, and smelled the rabbit.

"A little rabbit!" said Coyote, smacking his lips.

"You can't see me," said Little Rabbit. "It's dark. I'm sitting perfectly still like my mother told me to."

"I can see you," said Coyote, "and I will eat you!"

"Very well," said Little Rabbit, "but your belly will be so full of me that you can't eat the Big White Rabbit!"

"Big White Rabbit?" asked Coyote, greedily. "Where is the Big White Rabbit?"

"He sits outside the cactus den of the Hñuh, just over the hill," said Little Rabbit. "I saw him earlier this evening. He is very swift. You must go quickly and run fast to jump on him or he will get away!"

Coyote turned and ran fast to the cactus den of the Hñuh, just over the hill. There he saw a big white rabbit sitting in the moonlight. He ran and leapt high in the air, landing right on the white thing.

The white thing was clean cotton laundry, hung out to dry on a tuxwadá. Coyote landed on the white maguey and its sharp spines punctured a hundred little holes in him. He ran away yelping!

Little Rabbit's mother hopped home and Coyote never bothered them again.

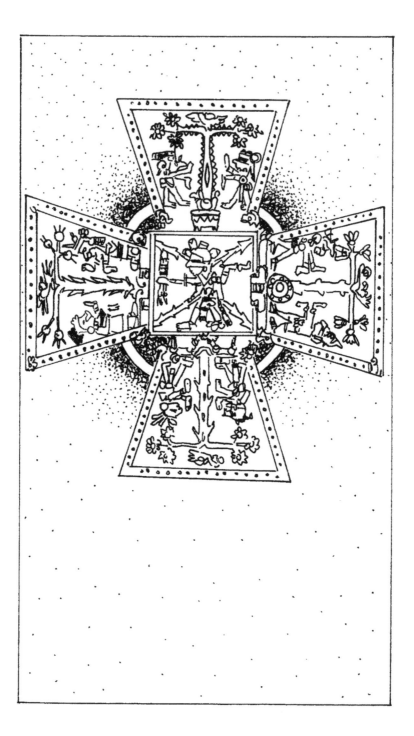

The Aztec Overlords of Zempoala

In the year we call 1480, the powerful Aztec Empire sent warriors to conquer their neighbors the Totonacs. The great Emperor of the Aztecs sent overlords and warriors to force the people of Zempoala to do as the Aztec Emperor wished. The Totonacs had to send him tribute, like taxes, every year. In what had once been a palace of the Totonac royal family, an Aztec overlord and his family and warriors lived in 1492. The Aztecs were homesick for the Valley of Mexico (where Mexico City sits now) and told stories from that region.

It was the time we call 9:30 at night, just before the Overlord's teenage children's bedtime. Young girls dressed in plain white cotton dresses, daughters of the Aztec overlord, sat on reed mats and listened to a storyteller. Their brothers, in loincloths and feather headdresses, sat behind the girls. Their favorite story was being told, a story that has many different versions because so many people have told it so many times. This story is an epic…it is very long…and it took the storyteller almost half an hour to tell aloud. Like many stories told by Native American people, this legend explains how some feature of the landscape came to be. This is a story about two mountains. And it is a love story.

The Smoking Mountain

Long ago, on the banks of the Great Lake in the center of the Valley of Mexico, there were four great kingdoms of the American Indian people known today as Aztecs.

To the north was the Black Kingdom, where the temples were painted black, and the warriors painted the top half of their faces black. These people were fierce and always ready to defend their homeland by war.

To the south was the Blue Kingdom, where the palace of the king was painted blue, and everyone showed hospitality to visitors from the other kingdoms. These people kept the peace by giving banquets and welcoming visitors from the other kingdoms.

To the west was the White Kingdom, where white snow covered the tops of some of the mountains, and white clouds hung in the western sky. These people defended their kingdom by their great religious faith.

To the east was the Red Kingdom, so named for the red sky of dawn in the east and the red flowers that bloomed there. These people remained strong by honoring family and keeping the kingdom together like a single plant with many flowers.

The four Aztec kingdoms shared in peace the Great Lake that both united and separated them.

The most beautiful girl in the Red Kingdom was the daughter of its king, a princess named Yoloxóchitl (Yoh-loh-SHOH-cheetl), which means Red Flower. Her father had forbidden her to marry until he found a young man that he thought was suitable for her. As you might have guessed, many young men came to ask his permission to marry Red Flower, but the king turned them all away. Yoloxóchitl was alone and lonely.

One evening Red Flower went for a walk from the Red Palace down to the banks of the Great Lake. The valley was surrounded by mountains except to the east where the morning sunlight poured in at dawn, red and beautiful. The rain and melting snow came down from the ring of mountains and formed the shallow lake in the middle of the valley. On the way to the lake, Red Flower walked through the market place of the Red Kingdom.

"Yoloxóchitl!" called the merchants seated on their woven reed mats. One merchant gave her a fresh-picked red flower to wear in her hair. A woman was grilling rattlesnake meat over a fire, and gave Red Flower a piece. Another gave her candy made from the dried pulp of a cactus. Everyone loved Yoloxóchitl like one big family.

Every morning, Red Flower's people, and the people of the other kingdoms, went out onto the lake in reed boats to catch fish. One of these boats was pulled up on the shore where Red Flower was walking. It was a warm day, and the breeze off the lake was cool. Knowing that all her people loved her and would deny her nothing, she borrowed the reed boat without asking anyone, and paddled out onto the cool lake.

It was evening, and the sun was in the west. The white clouds and the white, snow-covered mountains of the west shone brightly. There was in the center of the lake a small island. On it was a huge cactus where the Aztecs once saw an eagle sit eating a rattlesnake. In that place the Aztecs placed a paint-striped pole that served as the boundary marker where the four kingdoms touched. The pole was striped red, blue, white, and black, for the four kingdoms.

Yoloxóchitl paddled the reed boat around the island to start back home. Over the still water she heard someone singing on the western shore. It was the voice of a young man. Forgetting any danger, and against custom, Red Flower paddled past the painted boundary pole and headed toward the western shore.

As she glided into the shallow water, a young man stood up from the rock he was sitting on. He came down to the shore. He was the most handsome young man Red Flower had ever seen, and he wore a beautiful cape made of white bird feathers and the headdress of a prince. He greeted her very politely and pulled her boat onshore. She stepped out of the boat and onto the beach.

"I am Tépetl (TEH-pehtl)," he said, "Strong-like-the-Mountain. I am the prince of the White Kingdom here on the west bank of our lake."

Red Flower introduced herself, and told him how her father had turned all her young men friends away. Strong Mountain told her that his father had done the same, sending all his young lady friends away. The two talked quietly, as friends, and the evening passed quickly. As night fell, their hands touched. Then their lips touched.

Soon their hearts touched, and they were in love.

Strong Mountain asked Red Flower to marry him and she agreed. They went up the pathway to the White Palace of his father the White King. The two lovers passed tall pyramids and great temples to the Aztec gods. The tallest pyramid was the Temple of Quetzalcóatl (Keht-sahl-KOH-ahtl) the Feathered Serpent god.

In the presence of the White King, the two young royals bowed low. Strong Mountain explained that he had asked Red Flower to be his bride. He thought that his father could not object to his marrying a princess, but the king was angry that he had not been introduced to the princess before Strong Mountain proposed to her. The king refused to give his permission for Strong Mountain to marry Red Flower, and the prince became angry.

"I will leave this kingdom," he declared loudly, "and Red Flower and I will find happiness somewhere else!"

Even though they had known each other only a short time, the prince and the princess were deeply in love. The two young lovers left Strong Mountain's home and went back down to the beach. The moon had risen in the afternoon, and the lake was lit by moonlight as the sun set. They climbed into the reed boat and Strong Mountain paddled them past the painted pole to the opposite shore.

In Red Flower's kingdom the two went to the palace to see her father. She thought that he could not possibly object to her marrying a prince; after all, who could be more suitable? But her father became angry at her for ignoring the customs of her people and accepting Strong Mountain's proposal before her family had approved. He told Strong Mountain to return to his own kingdom.

Now it was Red Flower who stamped her foot with anger. "If he must leave this place," she said boldly, "then I will also go." The two left, hand in hand, and walked back down the path to the Great Lake. There they sat on the edge of the reed boat and talked.

"Let us go to the Black Kingdom in the north," said Strong. "I am a friend of the prince there. We played war games together as boys. I believe that they will welcome us."

So they paddled to the north, and when the moon was high they came to the shore of the Black Kingdom. Young warriors with the upper part of their faces painted black ran down to the shore and surrounded the two young lovers. As guards of their kingdom they wanted to know if the two in the reed boat were spies or enemies. The leader of the warriors was the prince of the land, and he recognized Tépetl. They grabbed each other's forearms in a two-handed greeting and the Black Prince led the two lovers to the palace to meet with the Black King.

Red Flower was frightened as they entered the Black Palace. The halls were lined with heads cut off of enemies. In the courtyard was a rack of skulls of enemies sacrificed to the Aztec god Tezcatlipoca (Tehss-KAHT-lee-POH-kah). She huddled close to Strong Mountain. The Black Prince introduced his friend to the king and they bowed low, but the king spoke to them firmly.

"Beautiful young people, this is a nation of warriors. Your fathers have forbidden you to marry. If I allow you to remain in my kingdom and to marry, either one of your fathers might be angry enough to make war on my kingdom. Worse, they might both attack at once, and divide my nation between them." Then he added softly, "That is what I would do."

He paused for a moment. "You are both fine young people, and I admire your courage. Sleep here and we will protect you for one night only. In the morning we will make human sacrifice in your honor, but afterwards I must ask you to leave my kingdom."

Yoloxóchitl said bravely, "We thank you for your kind offer. Please do not make any sacrifices in our honor. We shall leave now."

Sadly, the young couple thanked the Black Prince. With an escort of warriors armed with clubs edged with sharp obsidian glass blades, they returned to their reed boat. The warriors clasped Strong Mountain's hands in farewell, and the Black Prince gave Red Flower a kiss upon the cheek. It left a smudge of his black face-paint. She smiled and did not wipe it off. Then the warriors pushed the young lovers' boat out into the lake.

"Let us go to the Blue Kingdom in the south," said Red Flower. "Their hospitality is great, and they will make us welcome." They paddled across the lake from north to south as the moon was setting and the stars were coming out. They reached the Blue Kingdom in the deep of night, but the guards at the shore greeted them most kindly and escorted them to the Blue Palace. A polite servant awakened the Blue King.

The King met them in the hallway of the palace, and touched

their hands to his in welcome. They told him of their troubles. "I value hospitality above all else," said the Blue King softly, "and you may rest here as long as you like. But I cannot allow you to marry and be prince and princess in my kingdom. What would my own children think? Sooner or later, they would become jealous of the hospitality you were receiving, because your presence here would make their positions as princes and princesses less important. No matter how good a host I might be, someday your welcome here would wear thin."

Strong Mountain nodded slowly. The young lovers understood.

"But stay this night," said the Blue King. "We shall hold a late night banquet in your honor. I know you must be hungry." The young lovers were amazed at how quickly everyone in the palace got up to enjoy a banquet. There was every kind of food, sweet, hot, salty, sour, spicy. The cooks prepared all of Yoloxóchitl's favorites, everything from grilled rattlesnake to cactus candy! Strong Mountain and Red Flower thanked the Blue King for his kindness.

"We would not spend another minute in your home," said Strong Mountain, "knowing that it would someday lead to trouble for you and your children. We will go from this place."

The servants of the Blue King gave the two young lovers flowers, and food to eat in the boat. The King himself joined his servants and guards at the shore to wave farewell to Strong Mountain and Red Flower. The King and his servants carried torches to light the path down to the lake, and held the torches high as the lovers paddled away. The people onshore sang a song of farewell, and threw the torches high in the air as a salute to the Red Princess and White Prince. The torches sailed high and fell into the lake, hissing as they struck the water and burned out.

The night was dark again, with only stars to light the lake.

"Where will we go now?" asked Strong Mountain in the darkness. "These four kingdoms are all the world that we know." He paused a moment in thought. "We could each go back to our own palaces, and never see each other again."

"I would rather not live than live without you," said Red Flower.

Strong Mountain smiled. He felt the same, and had hoped that Red Flower would say that.

"Let us go back to my kingdom," said the princess, "and go up the path past the palace to the place where I like to sit, looking out over our valley, and think."

They pulled ashore in the Red Kingdom not long before dawn. Leaving the reed boat on the beach, they walked up a trail that bypassed the palace and wound on up the slope to the east. They reached the gap in the mountains and sat down to rest at the highest point. Red Flower was cold, so Strong Mountain built a small fire. As they sat warming themselves, Red Flower laid down to sleep. Strong covered her with his white feather cape. The smoke from the fire swirled around Strong Mountain as he sat quietly. The smoke curled up past his face.

The white clouds to the west rolled in over the lake until they stood beside the mountain pass in which the young lovers awaited the dawn. Out of the clouds came the great Aztec god Feathered Serpent. He was a giant snake, as long as twenty reed boats. His head was as big as a house, and he had a crest of huge white feathers around his reptile face. He came down from the sky and lay on the rocks, where he transformed himself into a man with a huge white headdress of the rarest feathers of the quetzal bird.

"Tépetl," said Feathered-Serpent-in-the-form-of-a-man, "This is the first night of your life that you did not come into my temple to burn incense. I was very worried about you, my dear friend."

Strong Mountain sighed, and greeted Feathered Serpent, the god of the west. He explained how he and Red Flower had fallen in love, and now found themselves outcast by the entire world that they knew.

"Great Feathered Serpent," prayed Strong-like-the-Mountain, "could you make one of the kings change his heart and accept us into his kingdom as prince and princess?"

Feathered-Serpent-in-the-form-of-a-man was silent for a moment. Then he spoke softly.

"I am sorry, Tépetl, but I am only a god. I cannot change what men and women feel in their hearts. Only men and women can do that for themselves."

Now Strong was silent for a moment.

"Then," he asked softly, "could you make it possible for Red Flower and me to be together...forever?"

Feathered Serpent smiled a sad smile. "Ah, Tépetl, my dear friend...that...I...can...do."

Feathered Serpent stretched his arms upward and the feathers of his great white headdress stirred in the dawn breeze. The great serpent uncoiled into its true form. Thunder rumbled and lightning flashed. The lovers were transformed. The great serpent raised its head up, up until it reached to the clouds, though its enormous tail still touched the earth. Then it pushed off from the earth, and its huge serpent body slithered up into the clouds.

Where the gap in the mountains had been, there now lay a huge new mountain, covered with a blanket of white snow. It looked like a woman lying on her side, covered with a white feather cape. The Aztecs of the four kingdoms awoke at dawn and gasped with surprise when they saw the new mountain.

"Ixtac cíhuatl!" they exclaimed (EESH-tahk SEE-wahtl), "A Woman Lying Down!"

Beside it was a huge new volcano that looked like a man kneeling down beside the woman, with volcanic smoke circling about his face.

The Aztecs of the four kingdoms pointed and gasped, "Pópoca tépetl!" (POH-poh-kah TEH-pehtl), "A Smoking Mountain!"

And there they sit, the snow-covered mountain Ixtaccíhuatl and the volcano Popocatépetl, century after century, looking down upon their valley kingdoms. I cannot say if mountains are able to be happy…but this I can say, my children.

They shall be together…forever.

A Poem From Texcoco

The story behind the poem: There were several Aztec Indian kingdoms in and around the Great Lake in the center of the Valley of Mexico in 1492. The city of Tenochtitlán (Teh-NOHTCH-tee-TLAHN), where the Aztec Emperor lived, was not the only capital city around the lake. Another capital of a small kingdom was the city of Tlacopán (Tlah-coh-PAHN), west of the lake. Still another capital was Texcoco (Tesh-KOH-koh), in the eastern side of the flat valley. (This was two hundred years after the events in the legend of The Smoking Mountain were said to take place.) These three cities, and the kingdoms of which they were the capitals, formed a triple union encircling the lake, which had come to be called Lake Texcoco. All three kingdoms were populated by Aztecs. The cities were friendly towards one another and so were their kings. Although there had been wars between the Indian kingdoms in the past, 1492 was a year of peace. The triple union of Aztec kingdoms is mentioned in the poem below as the "Three Thrones."

In Texcoco, there had been a great and wise king named Netzahualcóyotl (Neht-SAH-wahl-KOH-yohtl), or "Hungry Coyote." He lived from April 28, 1402 until June 4, 1472. He had been dead 20 years in 1492 and the poems and songs he wrote had been recited and sung everywhere Aztec people lived.

The storyteller in the Aztec overlord's home in Zempoala recited one of Hungry Coyote's poems that boys liked to hear. It's about fighting, and power, and friendship among warriors. Netzahualcóyotl wrote the poem…that he called a song…for a prince, a friend of his who was the son of the King of Tlacopán. In the poem, Hungry Coyote predicts that just as each person's life must end, so the glory of the three kingdoms must end. This is how much the teller in the palace of the Aztec overlord remembered of the long, sad poem, recited by the Poet to a princely friend while visiting in the prince's garden.

HUNGRY COYOTE'S LAMENT

I want to sing for a moment,

Since I have a moment to spend.

May my song be enjoyed by you,

If it is worth it, my friend.

And so I begin my song's intent,

But more than a song, it's a sad lament.

Now, my friend, let us be glad,

And enjoy the flowers that bloom,

And forget the troubles we've had,

And forget all our fear and gloom,

And in life's garden, my friend,

The sadness of life can end.

I shall sing the music of life,

And dance by the garden in leaf.

In the works of the Powerful God,

Be glad in the glory of belief,

For life here on Earth is so brief.

And is taken as if by a thief!

In this palace which is your own,

You have placed your noble throne.

Your kingdom shall grow, I believe,

Rejoice and do not grieve!

You are wise, Oyoyotzi'n (Oh-YOH-yoht-SEEN),

Famous prince, and a ruler unique.

Enjoy your garden today.

Someday it, in vain, you will seek.

Someday Fate will be cruel and devour

Your kingly wand, symbol of power.

The moon of your glory will set,

Your companions abandon you yet.

All the princes who rise from your nest

Like eagles today, will soon fall.

As their fathers before them now rest

In the poverty of death, so shall they all.

Your great deeds will only be memories,

Your glories and victories be past.

The joys of today flow as tears

To the ocean of darkness at last.

All of your royal family,

Who serve you with feathers and crown,

Will, after you leave life and them,

Suffer loss. Their heads shall bow down.

And All of this unique greatness,

Of our kingdoms, our crown and shield,

Fate and Time shall wear them down

Our Three Thrones their power shall yield.

In Tenochtitlán (Teh-NOHTCH-tee-TLAHN), the first king,

Motecuhzoma (MOH-teh-koo-ZOH-mah), of three;

Hungry-Coyote, I who sing,

Texcoco I oversee.

Totóquil (Toh-TOH-keel), your father well-known,

Is the third great king on his throne.

I fear not that the world will forget

Great deeds done in this wonderful place.

The Lord of the World, with his hand

Made things happen by his own grace.

Enjoy what you have! And with flowers

From this garden of life make your crown.

Hear my song. Hear my music these hours.

On borrowed time we live, then lie down.

All things in life are just borrowed.

It's not real, it will all pass away.

This is the truth…The great question

That we all must answer someday.

Where are the kings of days gone by?

And the flower warriors of the past?

Where are their voices, their deeds?

They rest in their graves at long last.

So, let us both now, on this day,

Befriend us and bind us together.

For the future will surely bring change,

As the winds bring a change in the weather.

SCARY AZTEC STORIES

The hour was late, but before they went to bed the sons and daughters of the Aztec ambassador in Zempoala wanted the storyteller to tell some of the scary stories that were everyone's favorite. The storyteller said he didn't know any scary stories. The Aztec teens begged! The storyteller was only joking. As the fire burned low he delighted them as he old two terrifying tales from the Aztecs of the Valley of Mexico!

The Wailing Woman
A Tale from Tenochtitlán

Once there was a widow woman of low birth who was poor but very beautiful. Her name was Squash Woman. She lived on the bank of the Great Lake by the causeway from the shore to Tenochtitlán on an island. Her husband had died falling off the causeway of Tlatelolco into the lake. He had been carrying a heavy load of fruit on a strap and when he fell the weight held him under until he drowned. With no husband to do the selling of their garden produce, the woman sold the family's squash in the marketplace with her two little sons.

One day, the woman was sitting in the marketplace with her children when a handsome prince of the Aztec Emperor's family came along, carried on a traveling chair by four slaves. The prince saw the beautiful widow woman selling squash. He ordered his slaves to stop and set down his traveling chair, which was called a litter. He stood up, stepped off his litter, and went to the woman.

He bought some squash and asked her to deliver it to a door to the kitchen in the palace where he lived, for he had no room on the litter to carry the fat squashes.

When the woman went to the palace at sundown, the servants invited her in. The prince had planned it this way.

She soon fell in love with the prince and they met many times, but he never really loved her. He was only toying with her affection.

At last she told the prince that she wanted to marry him and become his princess. The prince did not want to marry her, but he did not know what to say. Then he had an idea.

The prince told her, "I could not marry you because you already have children, and they would become little princes if you became a princess. This would offend the rest of the royal family because they would accept only little princes of whom I was the father."

Knowing that the woman loved her sons and could never give them up, he felt this lie would keep her from asking again.

Squash Woman left that night, and as she was walking to her home she crossed the causeway where her husband had drowned. She stood for a long time looking into the dark water. At last she made up her mind. She wanted to be a princess and, she thought, only her children stood in the way.

Back at the house, she woke the two boys and led them out to the causeway. They went to the spot where the boys' father had fallen in. She told her sons that the gods of the lake had asked them to come and live in the lake with their father.

Squash Woman threw her two children into the lake, and they drowned. The two boys went to the Heaven of the Rain God, where all drowning victims go, and where they found their father and were happy. But Squash Woman had been lying about the water gods. She had killed the children so that she could marry the prince.

The next day Squash Woman went to the prince and told him that she could now marry him. She told him the children would no longer stand in their way, because she had drowned them in the waterway of reeds.

When the prince heard this he was horrified and disgusted by what she had done. He told her she was an evil person, and he hated her. He would have had her executed for her crime, but he felt that it was his fault for lying to her about the marriage.

He turned the woman out, and told her never to come to his palace again. The prince went into the temple of his gods and prayed and burned sweet-smelling grass and begged for the gods' forgiveness.

Squash Woman went crazy. She had lost everything…her family…the man she thought loved her. She began to wander the night, crying for her lost children. Finally she grew old and died and went to the Land of the Dead. She did not find her children there for they were in the Heaven of the Rain God. She went to the Lord of the Dead, called Skeleton Man, and asked his permission to go back to the land of the living.

He was so tired of hearing her cry for her children that he let her go so that the Dead could have some peace and quiet. She crossed back over the Flint Road to the land of the living, but all her flesh had rotted off or been cut away by the sharp flint on the road to and from the Land of the Dead.

She came back to earth as a skeleton, her bones rotting and fleshless. She wore the same ragged, white cotton dress she had worn in life. She wandered all night along the causeways and beside the water, looking for her lost children.

Because she was dead, but back walking the earth, she became powerful like a goddess. She deeply regretted killing her children, and devoted all time to warning others who are about to do something evil. She can turn herself back into a beautiful woman and talk to you. But if you answer her, she might take your soul from you. You must avoid her like death itself. When she knows you cannot escape her, she turns from the beautiful Squash Woman into the horribly ugly skeleton she really is. She looks like the Lady of the Dead, the Skeleton Woman, wife of the Lord of the Dead.

Do not go out at night where you should not go. Do not go to get drunken on the corn beer. Do not be mean to your little brothers and sisters. Do not be rude to your elders. Do not steal. If you do, the Wailing Woman will come and get you!

She is the One-Who-Cries-at-Night.

And she brings death.

Skeleton's Revenge
A Tale from Tlacopán

The story behind the story: The Aztec people in 1492 had many of the same kinds of games as we have today. One of their games was called patolli (pah-TOH-lee). Because the game also had some religious importance to the gods of the Aztecs, the game was outlawed by the Spanish priests after 1521. Only in the Twentieth Century did some Mexican Indians admit that they still play patolli in secret. The game had a board similar to the modern Game of Life or to Parcheesi, but it was a gambling game. Players had to keep putting their bets into a pile to keep playing. The players threw dice made of human knuckle bones and moved painted squash seeds around the game board until someone got to the center square. The first player to reach the center square won all the things that had been wagered by the players.

Here is a scary story about a patolli game played in

Tlatelolco, one of the Three Thrones kingdoms, in a building along a causeway over the Great Lake. This is how the overlord's resident storyteller told it in the palace of the Aztec overlord of Zempoala.

A group of Aztec eagle warriors sat together in a room, gambling on a reed mat. The eagle warriors were the bravest and highest-ranking warriors in the army of the Emperor of the Aztecs. They played patolli, the game of beans given to the Aztecs by Five-Flower, the God of Gambling. The warriors wore flowers on their cotton garments and had long green quetzal feathers in their hair. They had gold earrings, gold nose rings, and gold cuffs like a wide bracelet worn on the muscle of the upper arm. With all their pretty finery you might think they were peaceful. You would be wrong.

Dead wrong.

Each warrior had a mace: a wooden club with a stone on the end for cracking open enemy skulls. Each one had a dagger with a wood handle and an obsidian blade; obsidian is a volcanic glass and is the sharpest substance known to man. An obsidian blade wears out quickly, but while it is freshly-made it is the sharpest thing there is. Each man had a bludgeon...a wooden club with rows of sharp obsidian blades set into it. The weapon crushed bones and slit flesh at the same time. They dressed in pretty clothing...but they were deadly warriors.

The warriors faced death on a daily basis, so no silly children's game satisfied them. They made huge, dangerous wagers, so the game would be as exciting as risking death and killing enemies in battle. They were so much in love with gambling that they bet more and more of their worldly goods with each throw of the human-knuckle-bone dice. An Aztec warrior might gamble away all his belongings, then bet his children and lose them, then bet his wife and lose her, and in one last attempt to win everything back, he would bet his own life into slavery. If he won, he got back all he had lost. If he lost, he had to become the slave of the winner, who could sell him in the slave market for silver, or gold, or trade goods.

Two men were the best players that night. One by one the other men had lost the colorful feathers from their warrior's hats, or the gold rings and bracelets from their hands, or their nose-jewelry, or their ear-plugs. One by one they dropped out of the game and left, until only two men remained.

They gambled and gambled. One man, a tall, dark-skinned warrior, was winning everything. The other, shorter man was losing everything.

The loser lost his cotton shirt, his jewelry, and all his belongings. Then he lost his house, his children, and finally his wife. In one last try to win everything back he bet his life against it all.

He threw the knuckle-bones in the air and clapped his hands, and called out the name of the god Five-Flower for good luck.

He lost.

Before he gave himself over to a lifetime of slavery, he told the winner of the patolli game that he wanted to go to a temple and pray for forgiveness for his foolishness. The tall man agreed, and said he would wait for the chubby loser in the room where they met to gamble.

The loser left the room where they had played patolli. He went out to the causeway and toward the temple. All the way to the temple, the loser was trying to think of something to do to win back his belongings. At the temple square there was a sacrificial stone, where a human sacrifice had been made. A flint knife still lay on the stone, covered with blood. It was not normal for a sacrificial knife to have been left behind. The short man took this as a sign from the gods.

He was to use the knife to get his belongings back! He took the knife and went back to the causeway where the tall man was waiting to take him into slavery. Since no one else had stayed at the game, only these two men knew who had won and who had lost.

The loser met the winner, and said he had forgotten to include this knife in the belongings the tall man had won. The tall man bowed politely and said the short man could keep it. While the tall man was bowed over, the short man raised the knife high, and plunged it into the skull of the winner. The tall man fell dead.

The loser rolled the dead man to the edge of the causeway, next to a stand of tall reeds in the water. He tried to pull the sacrificial knife out of the skull of the dead man, but it would not come out, no matter how hard he pulled. This was an evil sign, but the loser left the knife in the skull of the body and rolled it into the water.

He gathered all the tall warrior's winnings, which were wrapped in the chubby man's own cloak. The next day he told his friends that with the last throws of the bones he had won everything from the tall man. At last, he said, the tall man had bet his own life in slavery against all the other belongings, and lost. When he had lost the last bet, the short man said to his friends, the tall stranger had run out into the night.

Since no one saw the tall stranger for many months, everyone guessed he had run away to avoid becoming a slave.

The loser of that patolli game was wealthy now, with all the belongings of the dead man and all the other warriors' losses from that terrible night. He became famous in the town of Tlatelolco, where he lived. He bragged about what a good gambler he was, and laughed at others who had lost their goods in games of patolli. He bought some slaves and was mean to them.

One night, the rich chubby man was walk along the causeway headed to the gaming house, close to the stand of reeds where he had dumped the body a year before. It was a dark, starry night, and no one else was out walking at that hour.

Just then, the rich loser heard something in the reeds. Perhaps it was a duck he could catch and cook. He stopped and bent down, spreading the tall reeds with his hands.

What he saw was not a duck.

It was the tall man he had murdered a year before. The head and shoulders above the water were only a skull and a skeleton with almost all the flesh eaten away. Out of the skull stuck the stone knife.

The short warrior gasped at the sight…and the horrible smell.

The tall skeleton's left arm flew up out of the black water and grabbed the heavy man, holding him bent over. The skeleton's rotting right arm came out of the stinking water and pulled the sacrificial knife from the skull with no effort at all. The skeleton man drove the knife into the heavy man's skull.

The heavy man screamed and fell, dying, into the stand of reeds by the causeway.

No one heard him.

Farther along the causeway, men gathered in the gaming room to play patolli.

In the Ruins of Tajín

Only one hundred miles north of Zempoala, at another Totonac city named Tajín (Tah-HHEEN), meaning Thunder and Lightning, the events of many Totonac legends took place. Some Totonacs still lived among the ruins of Tajín in 1492. (Many other ancient cities were completely abandoned.) These Totonacs were poor farmers and were not under the control of the Aztec Emperor. El Tajín today is a Mexican National Park and a UNESCO World Heritage Site. Tourists come from all around the world to see an amazing and dangerous dance now re-enacted daily at El Tajín.

The Voladores

The story behind this incredible story: The most unusual ancient ritual of the Nahua, Otomí, Huastec, and Totonac People of Mexico is the Dance of the Birds, also called the Danza de los Voladores (VOH-lahd-THOH-rehss. The Flying Ones.) A very skilled man climbs a 90-foot pole using a waist rope (the way telephone and electric company linemen do today.) He carries a long rope on his shoulders. Starting at the top and working his way back down, he wraps the long rope around the pole in a special pattern to form ladder-like access to the top. Five men climb the pole lifting with them a barrel wrapped in ropes, a square frame of poles about 6 feet on a side, and musical instruments. On the top of the pole four men place the barrel with four long ropes wrapped around it.

The barrel is designed to sit there, atop the pole, and turn freely. The fifth man climbs on top of the barrel with musical instruments and no safety harness of any kind. The square frame of poles is hung below the barrel, horizontal to the earth, to guide the four wrapped ropes as they unroll off the barrel.

Each of the four other men loops his rope around his waist. As the fifth man on top of the barrel risks his life to dance and play a drum and a flute at the same time, the four men leap out away from the pole. The ropes slowly unroll from the barrel, and the men, hanging upside down, whirl slowly to the ground. After the amazing, dizzying and dangerous dance, and just before their heads slam into the earth (which would kill them) the four flyers turn rightside up and hit the ground running. The flute player climbs down last.

In ancient times, the four flyers were dressed as birds. Today the Totonac dress for this ritual consists of red pants with a white shirt, a cloth across the chest and a cap. The pants, cap and chest cloth are heavily embroidered by the flyer's wife or mother. The cloth across the chest symbolizes blood. The cap is adorned with flowers for fertility, mirrors to represent the sun and from the top of the cap fly multicolored ribbons representing the rainbow. Over the centuries, many men have died when something went wrong during the deadly dance… but the Totonacs and some of their neighbors repeat this dangerous, dangling-upside-down dance still today.

It was about 9:00 p.m. by modern standards on October 12, 1492, and only two old men were still up, tending the fire in a farm family's hut in the ruins of Tajín. They quietly told stories about the bygone days of the Totonac Empire. This is the story of why the Nahua, Otomí, Huastec and Totonac men still risk their lives to dance the sacred Voladores dance.

The Dance of the Birds

One year, long ago, a drought hit Tajín and Zempoala, two cities of the Totonacs. Crops withered in the fields and fruit died on the tree. The wells of the people dried up. Five of the bravest young Totonac men decided send a message, a great prayer, to the God of Fertility, called Xipe Totec (SHEE-peh TOH-teck) by the Aztecs. No one knows how they devised their plan to act out their amazing prayer, but they wanted to show their willingness to die to save their People.

The five went into the great tropical forest and found the tallest, straightest tree. They knelt all night beneath it asking the tree's forgiveness for what they were about to do. In the morning they cut the tree down with stone axes. The young men caught the tree as it slowly fell, and did not let it touch the earth. They carried it on their shoulders and set it upon tables of stone. They trimmed all the branches and peeled the bark. In the clearing in front of the pyramid called the Temple of the Niches they dug a narrow, deep hole, and brought the slick tree to it. They stood it upright so that its bottom slid into the hole, much as it had been when alive. They packed dirt around it so that it did not move.

The young men dressed as the four birds sacred to Xipe Totec, the parrot, macaw, quetzal and eagle, representing the four elements of earth, air, sun and water. They climbed the pole with long ropes and wrapped them around the pole somehow (We do not know for sure how the first dance looked.) The young men hung upside down as the fifth man played on top of the pole, risking his life even more than the others did. The young men whirled around the pole thirteen times each as their ropes unwound. Thirteen rounds by each of four young men totaled fifty-two rounds, the number of years in the Aztec calendar round, used by our Totonac People and all tribes who traded with the Aztecs.

Xipe Totec was so impressed by the prayer of the five young men that he sent down the rain and the cities were saved. The dance was recreated at Tajín every year in memory of the great event.

Onboard the *Santa María*

The flagship of Columbus' little fleet, as a group of ships is called, was the *Santa María*. She - ships are always called "she" - was owned by Juan de la Cosa (HWAHN deh lah KOH-sah), a man from the northern part of Spain known as Galicia (Gah-LEE-see-ah). She was equipped with a new kind of rope rigging and canvas sails that had just been invented. In the centuries before, ships used only one large sail; by 1492 ships had several sails of different sizes, which made it easier to steer the ship by turning the sails to catch the wind in different ways. She was the kind of ship that we call a carrack today, and made all of wood, like all ships in those days, with very ornate carving for decoration. She was called by her true name, *Santa María* that means "Holy Mary" or "Saint Mary," but sailors onboard called her by her nickname La Gallega (Lah Gahl-YEH-gah meaning "the Lady from Galicia") for the home region of her owner.

The story behind the story of El Cid: The Song of El Cid, or The Poem of El Cid, is an epic, a very long legend told in verse. Everyone from Spain in 1492 knew the story by heart. El Cid was a famous knight who had lived 400 years earlier (A.D. 1040 to 1099.) The epic poem has over three thousand lines and is divided into three parts called *cantares* (kahn-TAH-rrehss: "singings.") Very few people could ever recite the entire adventure poem by memory. A few *juglares* (hoo-GLAHR-ehss: oral poets) are said to have memorized it all, and were hired by rich people to perform it over a period of four hours a night for three nights! Many men learned to recite their favorite parts, handed down orally over the centuries. Each sailor in Columbus' crew would have recited his favorite part of the poem a bit differently since changes sometimes slipped into men's memories.

Today we might read a book several times, or watch a movie or TV re-run several times over the years. In a society where few people knew how to read, reciting and hearing favorite stories, songs, and poems over and over was always a pleasant pastime. To prepare you for the upcoming selection from the epic poem, here is a summary of the first part:

The Poem of El Cid

Historical background of the true story and Summary of the First Part of the First Cantar

Rodrigo Díaz de Vivar (Roh-DREE-goh DEE-ahss deh Vee-VAHR) was a nobleman who owned land and a castle in the far northern part of what is now called Spain. He lived from the year 1040 until 1099. He married a lovely lady named Ximena (Shee-MEH-nah) of Oviedo (Oh-vee-EH-doh), who lived from 1054 to 1115. Late in their lives they were King and Queen of Valencia, and she reigned alone as Queen from 1099-1102 after the death of Rodrigo. During fighting with neighboring kingdoms…which was common in those times… Rodrigo was knighted for his bravery and leadership by the elderly King of Old Castille. (There was not yet a single large nation named Spain. That did not come until Ferdinand and

Isabel's time.)

Sir Rodrigo ordered the cities he conquered to pay him taxes, as was the custom in those days. When cities inhabited by Muslims sent their taxes, the men who brought the gold would kneel before Rodrigo and kiss his gloved hand as a sign of respect. When they talked to him, they politely called him by the Arabic title as-Sid or Sidi. The word means "My Lord," which was a common way to address a nobleman in those days. When the elderly King heard of this, he ordered that everyone in Old Castille call Sir Rodrigo by this Arabic title, which became, in Spanish, El Cid.

When the elderly King of Old Castille died, his will divided his kingdom in half, one half for each of his sons. This led to bitter hatred between the brothers, and a cruel and violent civil war broke out as each brother tried to take all of his father's former land for himself. Each brother declared himself King and tried to kill the other.

King Sancho and King Alfonso fought each other bitterly. When open battles between armies failed to yield a winner, King Alfonso is believed to have secretly had his brother murdered so he could take all of Old Castille for himself. With King Sancho dead, King Alfonso tried to govern all the land that had been his father's. El Cid refused to swear loyalty to him unless King Alfonso swore that he had not murdered his brother Sancho. King Alfonso was insulted and angry; he refused to swear he was innocent. He probably was guilty. El Cid became an enemy of King Alfonso.

Alfonso banished El Cid from the kingdom, making him leave behind all his lands, his castle called Vivar, and everything he had. El Cid, a brave and loyal knight under King Sancho, was treated like a traitor by King Alfonso. That is where the long, long poem begins. In the Middle Ages people believed in signs and omens; El Cid was believed to have been born in a good (lucky) hour, and first buckled on his famous sword in another good hour. Everyone in the poem looks for good or bad omens, like which way a crow flies.

Aboard the Santa María, only two or three sailors were still awake three hours after sunset, at about 10:00 p.m. by the hourglass. One was the teenaged cabin boy Pedro de Terreros who was serving a few hours as the sailor who turned the hourglass. Although the hourglass was needed the most when a ship was sailing along to help figure time and distance, it was turned every hour even when the ship was at anchor. As he watched the glass, waiting for the sand to run down into the lower bell, waiting until time to turn the glass, the cabin boy listened to an older sailor who walked the decks as a night watch. The night watchman liked to recite this piece of the epic poem, because it mentioned the Church of Santa María, and he was on the ship named Santa María.

The Exile of El Cid

Tears fell from El Cid's eyes as he turned
   and looked back at his castle and land.

He saw doors left open, gates unlocked,
   and the perches of his hunting birds stand

Empty and still. No fur blankets
   on the porches, and his hunting birds gone.

No falcons, nor even a molted hawk
   as El Cid sadly turned and rode on.

El Cid gave a sigh of great sorrow.
   "Lord in Heaven," My Lord El Cid prayed,

"my enemies at the court of the king
   have left me by their lies betrayed."

His followers spurred on their horses,
   and for speed they let loose their reins,

as they rode from the castle of Vivar,
   a crow flying on their right eased their pains.

It was a good sign. But as they rode toward
   the town of Burgos, home of the King

A crow flying on their left was an omen
   of bad things the future would bring.

"Be merry," said El Cid to his best friend,
   Álbar Fáñez (AHL-bahr FAHN-yess). "We are in exile.

But we will return to Old Castille
   in glory in just a short while!"

My Lord Rodrigo Díaz entered
   the King's city of Burgos with ease.

His soldiers, with lances held high,
   with pennants that flapped in the breeze;

Sixty pennants held by sixty loyal men.
    The people of Burgos leaned out

of their windows to see the procession.
    Some cried, and one man did shout:

"What a good servant El Cid would be!
    His loyalty to his king would not swerve!

If only he had a king who wasn't bad!
    If he only had a good king to serve!"

The good people of Burgos would have asked
    El Cid to their homes if they dared.

But King Alfonso so hated El Cid
    that all the good people were scared.

The King sent out royal decrees
    with heavy wax seals attached.

The decrees warned if anyone invited
    El Cid under their roofs, which were thatched,

the foolish host's home would be taken away,
    his eyes be gouged out. He'd be killed,

and the King would pray that the host's soul
    would not get to Heaven as God willed.

These good Christian people of Burgos
    were sad, but no one dared say so.

El Cid, the murdered king's champion,
   stopped at an inn to see if his men could go

inside for supper. The doors were locked tight.
   No effort could open them wide.

They were locked up with bolts, left and right.
   Hungry knights could not go inside.

The Cid shouted, but no one dared answer.
   El Cid rode up and knocked with his boot.

The door remained locked shut and silent.
   But a brave little girl, resolute,

Came out from were she hid
   with a memorized speech for El Cid.

"You put on your sword in a good hour,
   But letters, sent by the king's power,

Hospitality to your men do forbid.
   We can't let you in, My Lord Cid,

Or the cruel king will gouge out our eyes,
   Take all our belongings, kill the host.

You gain nothing by bringing us blindness.
   Don't send to sorrow each suffering ghost.

Please leave! God reward you for kindness!"

The girl ran behind the inn, out of sight,
  And El Cid knew all she said was right.

He spurred his horse, turned back to the gate.
  They left the inn's courtyard riding straight

For the Church of *Santa María* in the city.
  El Cid knelt down and prayed for God's pity.

On his horse once again, with his followers,
  Out the gates of the city they went.

Over the bridge Arlanzón (Ahr-lahn-SOHN), to find
  A field where this night could be spent.

El Cid, who in an hour that was good
  Put on his sword, spent the night in this wood.

His faithful soldiers camped around.
  But for money no food could be found.

In Burgos lived one brave man,
  El Cid's kinsman, Martín Antolínez

  (Mahr-TEEN Ahn-toh-LEE-ness),

A soldier who thought up a plan
  To make up for King Alfonso's meanness.

He brought El Cid's men bread and wine.
  The bread was fresh; the wine tasted fine.

Cruel King Alfonso had said
  No one could sell El Cid supplies.

Martín didn't sell the wine and bread.
  He gave them as a gift! He was wise!

"If the cruel king finds out I've fed
  My lonely kinsman," Martín said.
There's only one thing I can do:
  Escape and go riding with you!
Rest tonight, in the morning say prayers.
  We're dead if we're caught unawares!"

In a good hour El Cid put on his sword.
  He said to Martín, the brave lancer
Who brought the men food from his hoard,
  And his kinsman was quick to answer.
"I've no gold by which I could afford
  To pay for your service and trouble,
Come with me and fight by my side
  And someday I'll pay you back double!"
With his friends and his men he did ride
  Faithful followers all, true and tried!

The cabin boy Pedro laughed at how both a prayer in the Church of *Santa María* and a clever trick by a faithful cousin got El Cid on the road safely. The watchman had only recited 56 lines…the complete three-part poem is an amazing 3,730 lines!

The Poem of El Cid II

Historical background of later events and Summary of the End of the Second Cantar

The story behind the next recitation of the poem: El Cid has many adventures and faces many dangers. El Cid returns in triumph to the royal City of Burgos, after a victory against enemies of King Alfonso. The King forgives him for his doubts about the death of King Sancho and welcomes him back. King Alfonso restores the land, castle and wealth to El Cid, and gives him a huge reward for his service and to pay his men with. El Cid repays his cousin Martín Antolínez back double, and honors Álvar Fáñez with a special duty. King Alfonso of Old Castille makes El Cid the new King of Valencia, the city El Cid has conquered. However, King Alfonso orders El Cid to give his daughters in marriage to two princes El Cid doesn't like, to create poltical alliances King Alfonso wants. El Cid's men decorate the palace in Valencia for the upocoming wedding of El Cid's daughters. El Cid spends a huge fortune on the event (the equivalent of millions of dollars today.)

Next Pedro the cabin boy began to recite his favorite verses about the triumphant return of El Cid and the marriage of El Cid's daughters to two Princes in the church called Santa María, the same name as the ship he's sailing on!

The Triumph of El Cid

[This poem was written a thousand years ago, and it cannot be translated without using many old words from the Middle Ages. If you don't know the meaning of a medieval word, the little numbers will guide you to footnotes after the verses.]

They at once began to decorate
  Valencia's palace halls;
The floors with carpets of purple
  and silk hangings on the walls.
Every guest would be delighted
  in this beautiful palace to dine.
The Cid's faithful knights all gathered,
  dismounted, and stood in a line.

The Princes of Carrión, two brothers,
  to come and be wed were invited,
The Princes rode straight to the gate,
  from their caps to their boots well bedighted. [1]
They entered politely and bowed down
  to El Cid, the Lord of the castle. [2]
Each greeted the Cid's lovely Lady,
  and saluted each knight and each vassal [3]
Who were seated on elegant benches.
  El Cid, born in a good hour,

Said, "It needs to be done, so let us do it!
   Álvar Fáñez, I give you the power,
Beloved knight, and I give you the honor!
   To each Prince give a daughter's hand!
Let us pray a benediction!
   This wedding the King does command!"

Álvar Fáñez was nicknamed Minaya.
   He took each lovely girl's hand,
And facing the Princes he ordered
   the two royal brothers to stand.
"On the word of Alfonso our King,
   these ladies Minaya does give
For the honor and good of us all!"
   The men's joy was superlative.

The Princes went to kiss the hands
   of El Cid and his lovely queen.
Then everyone leapt on their horses
   and in haste rode away from the scene
To the great Church of Santa María
   where Bishop Jerome did await,
Already robed in his vestments [4]
   just inside the churchyard gate.

He gave them his benedictions
  and sang them a holy mass. [5]

Then the wedding party cavalcaded [6]
  to Valencia's arena to pass

An afternoon of the jousting sport! [7]
  My Lord Cid and each knight running courses,

In sport with the newly-wed Princes!
  Three times El Cid changed horses!

He who in a good hour saw birth,
  Was pleased with his new sons-in-law!

They were horsemen and knights of great worth!
  To the feast did the riders withdraw,

To Valencia's beautiful fortress
  rejoining their ladies or wives,

For a glorious feast of the wedding!
  The next day El Cid contrives

Seven tablets to ride at and break [8]
  before the next feast can begin!

Two full weeks did the great celebration
  continue for El Cid and his kin!

After two weeks of great feasting
  for the Cid's noble guests did end,

Lord Rodrigo, the Cid, who was born
  in a good hour, gave gifts to each friend!

Of palfreys and mules and swift horses, [9]
    fine cloaks and furs untold, [10]
He gave each noble guest
    uncountable gifts of gold!
Even the Lord Cid's vassals
    gave a token to every guest. [11]
Whatever the nobles might want,
    in their hands very soon would rest!
All the guests bade farewell to El Cid,
    who in a good hour girded steel. [12]
All who came far for the wedding
    Were going home rich to Castille!

The guests bade farewell to El Cid
    and his vassals and to his wife.
The were grateful for being well-treated
    and shown the best time in their life.
The sons of the great Count Gonzalo,
    El Cid's two new sons came to call,
Diego and Fernando
    Were pleased the most of all.

For Castille the guests have departed.
    In Valencia stay El Cid and his wife,

And with his new sons and his daughters
  Live for two years of their life.

The residents of Valencia,
  a city and kingdom besides, [13]

Bestow favor upon El Cid's family [14]
  which now in their city abides. [15]

My Lord Cid and his vassals were joyful.
  Praise Saint Mary, and the King who said

The princes and the Cid's daughters
  for the good of all should wed.

With these final verses,
  this Second *Cantar* shall end.

May God and All the saints
  bless you, the listener, my friend!

WORDS YOU MIGHT NOT KNOW:

1. **bedighted**: elegantly dressed

2. **lord**: any noble person, or king, or owner of a castle

3. **vassal**: someone who takes an oath to serve a king or nobleman for his entire life

4. **vestments**: the beautiful garments worn by a church leader to remind us of the glory of God

5. **mass**: the ceremony of worship in the Catholic Church

6. **cavalcaded**: proudly rode on horseback in a long line like a parade

7. **jousting**: sporting horseback duels between knights in which no blood is to be shed

8. **tablets**: life size man-shaped wooden targets that shatter when hit dead center with a lance by a man on horseback; a rider must break the tablet to win the game

9. **palfreys**: a type of horse (not a separate breed) highly prized for riding in the Middle Ages, mules are good pack animals, and every nobleman and –woman went only on horseback, never on foot. The Spanish word for "gentleman" is *caballero* or horseback rider. Elsewhere in the poem we learn that El Cid's horse was named Babieca.

10. **cloak**: a heavy cloth cape for a man or woman, usually decorated with embroidery or gold

11. **token**: in the Middle Ages, any small gift

12. **girded steel**: buckled the belt (girded) on which his sword (steel) was suspended

13. **kingdoms**: during the Middle Ages, kingdoms were very small; Valencia is a city and a small kingdom of the land within ten or fifteen miles of the city

14. **bestow favor**: means to approve of, and support

15. **abide**: means to live in

On The Central
American Mainland

Maya Descendants

The great empire of American Indians called the Maya built huge cities, tall temples, and massive pyramids. They ruled southeastern Mexico and Northern Guatemala for a thousand years. By 1492, however, their huge cities were abandoned and their civilization had broken up into small cities and villages. The single empire became several ethnic groups spread from Yucatán in Mexico south to tribes in western Honduras. The great Maya cities of Calakmul, Tikal and Palenque and smaller ones like Bonampak, Altun Ha and Uaxactun had all been abandoned and taken over by jungle animals and plants. No one knows exactly why the Maya people left their large cities around the year we call A.D. 1000, but a few smaller cities were still inhabited in 1492.

Chichén Itzá (Chee-CHEN Eet-SAH) was still inhabited, but Columbus never met those people who lived far inland. The ruins of Chichén Itzá are in modern day Guatemala, and have been declared a UNESCO World Heritage Site. The ruins of Uxmal are located 62 kilometers south of the Mexican city of Mérida, capital of the Mexican state of Yucatán. The name Uxmal comes from the Yucatec Maya word *O'oxma'al* which means "the City Built Three Times."

In Chichén Itzá

In a simple thatched hut near the Pyramid now known as "The Castle" in Chichén Itzá, a family of Guatemalan descendants of the Maya sat around a pit fire and told stories on the night of October 12, 1492. It was late at night for them, about 10:00 p.m. by our standards, but they stayed up late to save their favorite story for last. The story tells of their old military ally and sister city, the Mexican Mayan city of Uxmal (Oosh-MAHL), which had ceased to be inhabited by about the year 1200. The name Uxmal means "Built Three Times." This is the story of how it was rebuilt one of those times by a clever, magical dwarf.

The Dwarf of Uxmal

In the town of Uxmal there lived an old woman who was an oracle. An oracle is someone who can predict the future. She was able to close her eyes and see what would happen in days to come. Everyone loved her, because she helped them by predicting when to store up extra food because a dry spell was coming, or when to repair the thatched roofs of the houses because a big wind and rain was coming.

She never married and she did not have any children. The people of the town loved her and begged her to marry, even in her old age, so that perhaps when she died her child could continue to predict the weather for them. Because she had special powers, she decided to have a child without a husband.

She went to the jungle and found an empty green turtle shell. From it she made a rattle. She shook the rattle and sang to the rhythm.

Her magic worked; a few months later, she gave birth to a tiny baby. The baby was green like the turtle shell, and had red hair. He was a dwarf, and never grew tall at all. Everyone loved the dwarf because he laughed and danced and entertained the children of the village. One day the Dwarf of Uxmal found a dried-out gourd that no one had eaten. He shook it. The dried seeds inside it rattled. He made the dried gourd into a rattle to play.

One day, he was singing and dancing and playing his gourd rattle, and the King of Uxmal walked by on his way to the temple. The king remembered an ancient prophecy, made long before even the dwarf's mother was born, that someday there would come to Uxmal a tribe of people who played the rattle, and they would make one of their number the new king.

Since the children were all making rattles so they could sing and dance with their best friend the little dwarf, the king was worried. The king thought the Dwarf of Uxmal was trying to take Uxmal away from the king.

The king then became angry. He couldn't hurt the Dwarf of Uxmal, everyone loved the little man. Since people in those days believed in magic, the King of Uxmal challenged the dwarf to a duel using magic.

The king set three challenges for the dwarf.

For the first challenge, he tested the dwarf's ability to see things that could not be seen by normal people. He asked the dwarf to say aloud the number of trees in the hidden garden in the king's palace. Since only a very few people were allowed in the palace, he thought the dwarf would not know. But the dwarf's mother could see things by magic, and she told him the number was seven. The dwarf told the king and the king became angrier. The judges of this magic contest agreed that the dwarf had won the first round.

For the second challenge, the king tested the dwarf's power over animals and plants. He asked the dwarf to find a turkey gobbler (a male) who could lay eggs. The king was certain the dwarf couldn't do that. Only turkey hens can lay eggs. The dwarf went to a friend of his who was very fat and had a pot belly...that was rare among Mayas. He asked the potbellied man to help, and of course the man did. The dwarf led the man to the palace of the king and said,

"I couldn't find a male turkey that can lay eggs, but I found a man who's pregnant! That's about the same thing, isn't it?" The crowd laughed and laughed. The judges gave the dwarf the second victory for his cleverness.

Now the king was so mad he could spit! In the third challenge, he wanted the dwarf to show endurance for pain and strength in battle. The king ordered an advisor named Saiya to cut a stick from a shagbark hickory tree and place it on the dwarf's head. Then he was ordered to use a sharp spearhead to break the stick in half. Everyone in the crowd groaned because they thought their little friend would be killed in this challenge.

Saiya placed a shagbark stick on the dwarf's head and raised his a spear with its sharp flint point. He slammed the sharp edge of the spear point down on the stick. The stick was cut in half, and the dwarf, who was born by turtle magic, was not harmed. The judges knocked on the dwarf's head and found it as hard as turtle shell!

The Dwarf of Uxmal now demanded that, to be fair, the king undergo the same test of strength. The judges ordered the king to agree, and the king's skull was split open and he died. The dwarf became King of Uxmal! The children danced in the streets and shook their rattles. The prophecy had come true.

By his magic, the Dwarf King rebuilt the city.

He built the Pyramid of the Magician, so named because he used magic to build it. He built himself a new palace called Palace of the Governor, or Ruler. For his dear old mother he built a beautiful palace just for her. Today it is called the Palace of the Elderly Mother.

And that is the story of the magical Dwarf of Uxmal as told by the Yucatec Maya of Chichén Itzá!

On the North American Mainland

The Mocama

On the coast of what we now call Florida, along the Atlantic shore of the northern half of the peninsula, a tribe of American Indians called the Mocama (Moh-KAH-mah) lived. They were the Eastern Band of the Timucua, a tribe that no longer exists. They lived along the shore from the Saint Marys River to the area around the mouth of the Saint Johns River. In 1492, there were more than thirty-five Timucua chiefdoms with several hundred villages and over 100,000 Timucua people living in North Florida. Columbus never met these people. We know those who lived on the Atlantic shore called themselves Mocama, because the Spanish established a mission for them by their name, called San Pedro de Mocama in 1587. We do not know exactly by what name the entire Timucuan People called themselves; the name Timucua was given to them by the Spanish in the 1500's.

The Mocama Band of Timucuan men and women were very tall, taller than other tribes, and taller than the Spanish of 1492. The men tied their reddish-black hair in a bun on top of their head to make themselves look even taller to their enemies. Both men and women, and even children, were tattooed. Men earned their tattoos by deeds of bravery in hunting or in battle. People of higher social rank had more elaborate tattoos, made by poking holes in the skin with a thorn and rubbing ash into the holes. This was painful, and a test of bravery.

As impossible as it may sound, the Timucua women made clothing woven out of the long strands of the tree saprophyte known as Spanish moss. The moss was dried to make it stronger.

The men wore animal skins for clothes, and smoked tobacco in pipes with a stem of reed and a bowl made of dried clay.

The Timucuan houses were round and made of timber with roofs made of palm fronds. Their villages inland were protected by a palisade – a wall of posts planted in a circle around the village. The posts were too high to climb over and too close together to get through. An enemy might shoot arrows in, but he couldn't get in close for a kill with a club. Hitting with a war club was a typical way of killing in battle.

The Timucua raised maize [corn], beans, squash, pumpkin, and melons in fields and gardens. They hunted, fished, and even killed alligators. They had long-distance trade with the Mound Builder People of Cahokia (in modern Illinois) and as far north as Lake Superior. The main item they traded to get was ornamental copper, which has been found in house remains and graves, and analyzed as to its place of origin.

The tribe died out in the early 1800's and was absorbed into the Seminole Tribe, so it is difficult to know what stories they told. The Mocamas spoke their own dialect of Timucuan, which is related to Taíno, so they likely told the same kinds of Caribbean stories told by the Taíno. Here is one of those stories they may have told.

The sailors on Columbus' ships would have called this hour "the eleventh hour after high noon." The Mocama Band of the Timucua People were in their huts for the night. Only two were awake: a woman and her daughter were staying awake caring for the father in the family. He had been bitten by a snake while hunting. If he made it through the night he would live. The woman, his wife, was telling the young girl a story about the beginning of the world according to Timucuan beliefs.

The One-Legged Beings

Every creature that swims, walks, flies or crawls has a purpose
in the world, even the snake. Yaya, the Spirit of Spirits, the Maker
of All Things, made the world and all creatures who live in it. First
Yaya made the water, then up out of the water rose the land. The
mountains grew and caves formed.

Yaya called all the animals out of the Black Cave, two-legged birds, four-legged dogs, six-legged bugs, eight-legged spiders, many-legged centipedes and no-legged snakes. All these beings found homes for themselves, and food to eat.

Yaya saw that something was wrong. The land was dissolving into the water. The land was slowly shrinking.

Yaya put swimmers in the water, and told the swimmers to push against the land and hold it together so it would not slowly dissolve into mud and slip into the water. The swimmers tried, but they couldn't keep the land together.

Yaya was troubled. He had made the two-legs, the four-legs, the six-legs, the eight-legs, the many-legs and the no-legs! What else could he make?

There was one number of legs he had not used.

One.

Yaya made the one-legged beings.

He made them to stand all their lives in a single spot, without moving or speaking. Their branches above the earth gave shelter and shade and leaves for weaving and fruits and nuts to eat. Below the earth the one-legged beings have roots that spread out and hold onto the land.

The one-legs, Yaya's finest creation, held the land together. The wind could not blow the land away. The water could not wash the land away. The one-legs held the land in place! And the People came out of the Black Cave to live and be happy.

Every part of the one-legs is useful to the People. Wood, pith, leaves, branches, roots, sap, and bark each have their own uses. The little one-legs, grasses and plants, are just as useful. From the stem and root of a purple flower, the People make a paste to draw the poison out of a snake bite. You must always respect every one-leg, large and small, short and tall. Never pick them, or break them, or cut them down for no reason. They are our greatest friends.

The Mocama woman used a poultice...a sort of paste...of a purple flower's root and stems and her husband was cured of the snake bite.

On the South American Mainland

The Caribs

On the northern coast of South America, on the Atlantic shores and deeper inland in the jungles, lived a tribe of American Indians whom Columbus named the Carib (Kah-REEB). Modern Caribs hate that name and don't use it anymore. They call themselves by several different tribal names depending on where they live. One group is the Kalinago (KAH-lee-NAH-goh.) The Columbus-given name Carib would eventually also be given to the sea between the islands visited by Columbus and the mainland of South America; it is called the Caribbean. (Columbus did not meet any Kalinago people on his First Voyage, but he saw Caribs living on islands in the Caribbean during his Second Voyage 1493-1496, and met Caribs living on the coast of South America on his Third Voyage 1498-1500.) The Caribs were the enemies of the Taíno people on the island of Guanahaní, where the *Niña*, *Pinta* and *Santa María* were anchored on the night of October 12, 1492.

On the South American Mainland, three Kalinago men sat around a fire at midnight, acting as night watch for their village. (They lived on the Atlantic shore of modern Venezuela between Punta Piedras and Punta Calera in the modern Estado de Trinidad). The Kalinago were warlike people and had to protect themselves from their enemies. As they sat near the fire, one of the older men began to teach a teenage warrior Kalinago history with a story from the mainland jungles, the story of the origin of all jungle food Kalinagos enjoyed. One older man said it was the tapir who kept the food source a secret; the man telling the story was sure it was the rodent called the agouti (ah-GOO-tee).

Tamosi and the Tree of Life

Tamosi Kabo-tano (Tah-MOH-see KAH-boh TAH-noh), the Ancient One of Heaven, the Supreme Being, created the Forest World and everything in it. In the center of the world he planted a great Tree of Life. From it grew everything the people and animals needed to live. All they had to do was find it.

In the beginning of the Forest World, the Kalinago People had very little to eat. Tamosi had created them, but he expected them to get along on their own. The People had not yet learned to plant the cassava root to make bread. The People did not eat the animals in those days because the animals could still speak. The animals and birds also had very little to eat. Everyone was hungry.

But one little animal, the agouti, a large forest rodent, seemed sleek and fat and healthy. He went out every morning, far away into the forest. When he came back in the evening he seemed to have eaten. He dropped banana skins, cane strips, and other things the people and animals had never seen. The people and animals called a council and spoke to each other. They decided that the little agouti must have found a place where there was plenty of food to eat.

They decided to send one animal to follow the agouti when he went out the next morning, to see where he went, and come back and tell the rest of them. They sent the snake.

The snake waited for the agouti to pass by on his morning journey, and then he followed the little rodent a long, long way into the forest. The snake saw the agouti stop and look back to see if anyone was following him. The snake became afraid that he had been heard rustling among the leaves. He stayed behind, and the agouti went on. The snake had nothing to report, but the agouti came back looking well-fed again that evening.

The next morning the people and animals selected the woodpecker to fly above the forest floor and watch the agouti from above. The agouti looked around and did not see or hear anything following him on the ground. But the woodpecker saw some bugs in the bark of a tall tree, and he could not help but peck on the bark a little bit to get some of the bugs to eat. The agouti heard the woodpecker and suspected he was being followed, so he picked up some bitter weeds and pretended to chew them as if they were what he ate.

The woodpecker reported back to the people and animals. They found and tasted the bitter weeds and knew they had been fooled by the agouti.

The next day the people and the animals sent the rat to follow the agouti. Brother rat is the most sneaky and quiet of all the animals. He has to hide from people and meateaters all the time, and he can move more quietly than anyone else.

The agouti never knew the rat was following him. He stopped and looked all around and listened high and low, and when he could not hear or see anyone following him, he went to his secret place.

Brother rat followed.

The agouti went to the Tree of Life deep in the forest and gathered all manner of fruit from the ground underneath the tree. It was a most wonderful tree! Every fruit grew on its branches: bananas, plums, mangos, papayas. Every good root grew at the foot of the tree: cassava, yucca, yams. Every good berry and bean grew under its leaves, and every good grass and grain grew from its bark.

As soon as the agouti had eaten his fill, he wiped his face with his paws and went away.

The rat came back and told the people and the animals what he had seen. The rat led them all back to the tree. By the time they reached the tree, many more ripe fruits and other good things had fallen to the ground. They picked these up and ate them. After everyone was full, they talked about how to get more fruits and food down. No one could climb the tree; it was too big and the bark was too covered with plants they did not want to damage climbing over them.

After much talking, they decided to cut the tree down so they could reach all the fruit and berries and food growing on it, and dig up all its good roots to eat.

The people and the animals went and got stone axes and began to cut. They cut for ten days, but the tree would not fall. They cut for another ten days, and still the tree would not fall. By now they were very hungry again, and very thirsty. The people got calabash gourds off the lower parts of the tree and cut them open to make watercarriers. Each animal was given a gourd to carry water in, so everyone would have something to drink while they worked.

But the agouti, who had come upon them cutting the tree on the second day, was sternly lectured for being so greedy and keeping the tree to himself. Everyone scolded him, especially the monkey I-arreka-ru (EE-ah-REHK-ah-roo), who chatters and scolds everyone even today. When all the animals were given gourds to carry water in, they gave the agouti a basket woven of grass so he couldn't get much water, as a punishment.

After ten more days of cutting, the tree fell at last.

The people took away as their fair share what they still plant today: cassava, cane, yams, bananas, potatoes, pumpkins and watermelons. The animals took what they wanted: the birds took seeds, the rodents took grains, some of the others wanted green leaves, and so on.

The agouti was just getting back from the river, carrying his grass basket without much water left in it. When he got back only one kind of fruit was left. No one had taken the plums, so they became the food of the agouti.

The Tree of Life was gone, but its fruits and seeds filled the forest and fed all the people and animals…who are just people who can't talk anymore.

Tamosi and the Big Canoe

Tamosi Kabo-tano, the Ancient One of Heaven, the Supreme Being, created the Forest World and everything in it. One day long ago he came out of the Forest and spoke to his People. He told them a storm would come and so much rain would fall that water would cover the world. He told the People to cut the biggest tree and dig out a canoe big enough for everyone to ride in.

Most of the People did not believe this was possible and went about their daily chores. Only four married couples agreed to obey. They found the biggest tree in the Forest World, and cut it down with stone axes. They trimmed the branches off and used fire and stone adzes...the kind they used to hoe their gardens...to hollow out the tree into a canoe big enough for all of them to ride in.

They made a thatched roof over the canoe, and loaded dried gourd ladles to bail rain water out.

The eight people loaded into the big canoe a mated pair of every land animal, and gathered seeds of every good forest and jungle plant.

Dark clouds formed and a storm blew in like a hurricane. It rained and rained and rained and rained. Rivers overflowed their banks and the water rose above the treetops. The People bailed the big canoe to keep it afloat.

When the storm stopped, the water slowly ran back into the rivers and the big canoe eventually settled in the mud. The People looked out at the hurricane's destruction. The people looked out at the world swept bare by storm surge.

"Where are the hills to grow our crops on?" asked one man.

"Where are the trees to give us wood and fruits?" asked another.

"Where are the palm trees with leaves to make baskets and thatched roofs and body paint?" asked the third man.

"Where are the clear streams we drink from and fish in?" asked the fourth.

Tamosi Kabo-tano put everything back in its place, and the People were happy.

And we are happy still today.

On the Canary Islands

The Canaries are a chain of seven small islands in the Atlantic about 62 miles west of the mainland of Africa, about even with the modern boundary between Morocco and Western Sahara. Columbus' three ships harbored there in August, 1492, at the island of La Gomera (Lah Goh-MEH-rah), the fifth Canary island counting westward from Africa. Columbus and his men sailed into the harbor at San Sebastián (Sahn Seh-bahss-tee-AHN, the capital of the island) and stayed on La Gomera from August 12 to September 6, 1492. They made friends there as the sailors repaired and refitted the three ships. Those friends also told stories on this historic night, but it was already very early October 13 on the Canary Islands.

La Gomera has a mysterious history. The Canaries have been inhabited for less than three thousand years. No one knows when the original natives reached the Canaries, nor where they came from. The native people, called Guanches (GWAHN-chehss), spoke a language that had much in common with the Berber language from North Africa. Some mainland farmers from the Moroccan region of Gomara were probably brought to the Canaries, possibly by King Juba II of Mauretania, and named the Island of Gomera after their homeland Gomara.

Beginning long before the birth of Christ, the Canaries were visited over the centuries by sailors from the ancient empires of Rome, Greece, Phoenicia [Sidonia in the Old Testament; modern Lebanon] and Carthage (which was near the Mediterranean Coast of North Africa.) Catalán-speaking voyagers from the Spanish island of Majorca (Mah-YOHR-kah) settled the Canaries in 1312. The Canaries became a part of Spain in 1402, although inhabitants on some islands resisted until 1495. When Columbus landed at La Gomera in 1492, he was safely in Spanish territory, and he himself was almost certainly a Catalán speaker, so he felt right at home.

Now, on the early morning of October 13, 1492, some inhabitants of the city of San Sebastián de la Gomera were up before dawn. One was a *forner de pa*, a baker, as said in Catalán. He had to mix the flour, water and yeast, with a pinch of salt and a pinch of herbs in a dough, and let the dough rise for an hour before baking it in the oven. The delicious herb bread he made was very much in demand, and customers would be at his *forn de pa*, or bakery, at dawn to buy bread for the day. The forner had a daughter and a son who both helped him. As they worked and waited for the ovens to heat and the bread to rise, he told them old stories about the Canaries and about Gomera. Some were legends from the Middle Ages, others were two-thousand-year-old myths told since the time of the Ancient Greeks like the story about Hercules.

Scylla and Charybdis

The story behind the story: Everyone in 1492 knew the two-thousand-year-old myth, but here's a summary for teens today. In the centuries before the birth of Christ and the start of our current calendar, sailors on the Mediterranean Sea often told myths to explain natural dangers and to warn other sailors. Ancient Greek and Phoenician ships often sailed between the southern tip of Italy and the Island of Sicily. Tall rocks on the shores of the two land masses were called the Pillars of Hercules. So many ships sank in the turbulent waters between Italy and Sicily that sailors imagined huge monsters were to blame. One monster, they said, was named Charybdis. She lived underwater and when she opened her gigantic mouth the sea began to run down into it. Just as water draining from a sink will whirl, water going into her mouth formed a huge whirlpool that broke ships apart and sank them. Charybdis swallowed up the sailors and spat out the shipwreck debris. Scylla was a many-headed monster that lived on land and gobbled up any sailors who survived the whirlpool and swam to shore.

As ships traveled farther west in the Mediterranean, they came to the Straits of Gibraltar between Spain and Morocco where the calm, warm Mediterranean meets the cold, stormy North Atlantic. Dangerous currents there reminded sailors of the whirlpools hundreds of miles behind them at Sicily. In their minds, the home of Scylla and Charybdis moved westward to the waters around Gibraltar. Everyone in 1492 knew this old myth, but didn't really believe it anymore. However, it made a good story! The *forner de pa* on La Gomera called the mythic hero Hèrcules and called the story:

The Dark Sea

The ancient sailors from Carthage, Greece, Rome and Phoenicia sailed all corners of the Mediterranean Sea, but very few were brave enough to come out into the Dark Sea beyond the Pillars of Hèrcules. The Pillars were the huge rock now called Gibraltar on the north and Mont Abyla in Morocco on the south. The Atlantic was called the Dark Sea. In much of the Mediterranean, the water is so clear and shallow that the white sand at the seabed was almost visible, making the water a beautiful light blue color. In the Atlantic the water is several miles deep in places, and the water was a dark and frightening blue to ancient sailors.

Where the warm Mediterranean Sea touches the cold Atlantic Ocean, there were powerful currents in the waters between Spain and Morocco. As the Atlantic tide rises and falls each day, water churns around the island of Gibraltar. These strong currents sank many ships. If sailors saw a whirlpool they called it *La Caribdis*! If they saw a coastline that was rocky, with crashing waves that could break up a ship, they called it *La Escila*! Those who made it safely into the Atlantic in ancient times were often caught by the powerful current that sweeps southwesterly past the island of La Gomera. Any ship whose sails where torn by a storm, and could not use the wind to steer them, would be carried past the Canaries and out into the Dark Sea, never to be seen again.

Sailors from the Mediterranean began to say the Atlantic Ocean was the home of every kind of terrifying sea monster that destroyed ships and devoured their crews. The monsters tore the ships apart and chewed the pieces. Just like children will gobble up their bread!

The Ghost Island

The Island of Gomera became part of the Kingdom of Seville in 1485. In treaties signed by the King of Castille, he said he took dominion over "...the islands of Canaria, already discovered or to be discovered ...". He wrote this because of a strange series of reports of an eighth Canary Island, due west of La Gomera, out beyond the island Ferro, farther out in the Atlantic. How could sailors not know if there was an eighth island?

The Ghost Island sinks into the sea!

Sometimes the phantom island, surrounded by mist or fog, can be seen even from the highest point on La Gomera. When a ship sails toward the Ghost Island, and sailors see distant shores, mountains and valleys, the mist closes around the island and it disappears. The mist clears and there is only open ocean.

The island is called San Borondón by the people of the Canaries. Some old sailors even tell that they made it to the island and explored it some before it sank into the sea and they swam back to their ship. The fact that people offer sailors a drink of wine as payment for telling this story may have had some effect on the sailors' memory.

I, myself, have seen the island…and for a glass of wine…I'll tell you my story!

The Lady with the Candle

The baker slid loaves into the oven to bake as he told this story that happened, he told his children, exactly one hundred years before, in 1392.

The Canaries were settled in 1312 by sailors from the Spanish island of Majorca. They brought Christianity and the Catalán language with them. Over the years, numerous ships came to the Canaries from Majorca, and some sank in storms off the coasts. On the Island of Tenerife, in 1392, two Guanche goatherders walked along the beach named Chimisay, looking for a lost goat. The Majorcans had only been on the Canaries eighty years, and many Guanches did not know much about Christianity yet.

On the shore the young goat herders found a stone statue of a woman carrying a candle. It could not have washed up from a shipwreck, it was too heavy. This frightened them. They decided the statue must have come to life and walked up from the bed of the sea! Thinking the stone carving was a small sea monster, one boy threw a rock at it. The rock missed and the boy's arm was paralyzed. The other boy drew his knife and tried to stab the statue, but he couldn't make his arm work right, and ended up stabbing himself. The boys told Acaymo, the local mencey (MEHN-seh-ee, chieftain.)

Because they knew almost nothing about the Majorcan's Christianity, they decided the stone lady was Chaxiraxi (CHAH-shee-RAH-shee) the Mother of the Gods in the native pre-Christian religion. The chieftain put the statue safely in a cave called Chinaguaro (Chee-nah-GWAH-roh) to protect and perhaps worship it.

A Guanche named Antón (Ahn-TOHN), who had been taken to Castille, returned to the Island of Tenerife as a converted Christian. He saw the statue the Guanches were calling Chaxiraxi. He saw the face, the clothing style and the candle carved of stone that the Lady held in her hand. He recognized the statue as an image of Mary the Mother of Christ.

He told the mencey that the statue was not to be worshipped, but honored as a reminder of God caring for His people. The statue was moved to the cave of Achbinico (Atch-bee-NEE-koh) and honored there as Our Lady Candelaria, or Our Lady the Candle Bearer. By some miracle, the statue must have come by ship from a Catalán-speaking region. The ship must have sunk and the statue somehow brought up on the sand. The Lady was painted with dark skin color, and was carved with clothes very similar to those of Our Lady of Lluch (the patron saint of Majorca) and the Our Lady of Montserrat (the patron saint of Catalonia on the Spanish mainland.)

The statue now represents the patron saint of all the Canary Islands, Our Lady Candelaria.

The Dragon's Blood Tree

The baker and his children began to pull loaves of herb bread out of the oven as customers started arriving, but the baker told two more stories as he took customers' money and handed out bread:

On the Island of Tenerife, in the town of The Vines (Los Vinos), stands the oldest tree in the world…well, one of the oldest. The great and ancient tree, when cut, does not drip sap, it drips thick, red dragon's blood. This is how the dragon trees came into being.

The great mythical superhero Hèrcules was deeply troubled by violence in his kingdom of Thebes and a fit of madness caused by an angry jealous goddess. In a fit of rage he killed his own children. To redeem himself, and be forgiven by his people, Hèrcules went to the Oracle at Delphi who should see the future in fits of her own. Shaking the golden throne on which she sat, the Oracle ordered Hèrcules to go to the King of Argos, who had sent his sailors throughout the known world and knew where all the great cities and treasures of the world were kept.

The King of Argos assigned Hèrcules twelve impossible tasks to accomplish. One by one, with his incredible strength, Hèrcules finished each task and reported back to the King.

The eleventh impossible task was to go to the Garden of Hesperides, located in southwest Spain at the western edge of the known world in ancient times. In the garden there was a tree that grew golden apples, and the King of Argos wanted a basket of them.

When Hèrcules got to Spain, he found that the garden was guarded by a dragon with one hundred fierce heads. One hundred was a popular number of heads for monsters to have. The dragon with two hundred eyes was named Ladon, and he could see in all directions, so no one could sneak up on him and steal the golden apples.

Hèrcules was so strong he didn't need to sneak up. He fought Ladon and killed him. The dragon's blood poured out like a river, and bathed the roots of the tree of the golden apples. The trees no longer grow golden apples, but some of those trees were brought to the Canaries.

And if you cut their bark…they bleed red dragon's blood!

The Fortunate Isles

In ancient times, the seafaring people of the Mediterranean believed that far to the west, in the Atlantic Ocean, lay a chain of islands called the Fortunate Isles. When heroes and sailors reached the end of a dangerous and difficult life, they went to the Fortunate Isles and were happy forever.

The great Greek writer Plutarch said the breeze was always cool, the rain was only a silver dew in morning, and the trees bore delicious fruit for the residents of the isles, and the people there felt truly blessed on the Fortunate Isles.

Surely our beautiful Canary Islands are the ancient and mystical Fortunate Isles!

On The Atlantic Shore of Portugal

Along the Atlantic shores of the small kingdom of Portugal, in 1492, there were many little villages and towns. Most of the families in these villages made their living from the sea. A few adventurous men sailed on ships that traveled south around Africa and east to India, China and Japan. Other families sent their fathers and brothers and sons out to fish for a living. In these families, the women and girls sewed the daily clothes for the fishermen, prepared their meals, helped clean and dry the fish, or wove warm wool clothing to protect sailors from the cold winds at sea.

Men and boys repaired their fishing boats, tied cord into fishing nets and repaired the nets when they broke, and cut and sewed the canvas sails. Before going out to fish at dawn, each small fishing boat had to be made ready. In the predawn darkness, men sat tying new knots and repairing the fishing nets for the day's catch.

The sun was about to rise on October 13, 1492, ending the historic night at the island of Guanahaní. Back in Portugal, men and boys worked to ready their boats to sail out and catch fish at dawn. As they worked on their nets, fathers amused their sons with ancient stories.

The Iron Dancing Shoes

One day long ago, Princess Branca came to her father the King of Portugal and asked for a new pair of dancing shoes. The princess danced so much that she wore out a pair of dancing shoes every day, even Sundays! King Sancho the Eleventy-Leventh became angry because he had to order new shoes for her every day, and the royal shoemakers could hardly keep up with the demand. Thinking he could solve the problem, the king ordered that seven fine pairs of dancing shoes be made, but that they be made with soles of iron so they would never wear out.

The royal shoemakers and the royal blacksmiths worked together and made the finest dancing shoes ever. They were decorated with silver and gold, and lined with silk. But their soles were made of iron, to last forever. Sure enough, the next day the princess came back and wanted new shoes. She showed the old shoes, and their iron soles were worn completely through!

The king ordered more iron shoes to be made. But secretly he wondered what the princess was doing to wear out shoes so fast. He gave his advisors a secret decree, stating that any man who could discover how the princess wore out those shoes could marry the princess and become a prince.

That very same day, a sailor from the Atlantic shore came through the royal city. There he saw two foolish men hitting each other over and over again.

"Why are you two hitting each other?" asked the sailor.

"We are fighting over a cap," said one of the men, and he hit the other.

"If it means so much to you," said the sailor, "you may also take my cap, so that each of you may have one."

The two men stopped fighting. "No, no," said the other. "We must have this cap." He held up a bright red and green cap with a bell on its point. "This is a magic cap. When our father, the magician, died, he left this cap to whichever son is the smarter of the two of us."

"What does the magic cap do?" asked the sailor.

"If the wearer says, 'Cap, cap, cover me up,' the wearer becomes invisible," answered the other.

"I have an idea," said the sailor. "I will take this orange from my sack and throw it a great distance. Whoever reaches the orange first and brings it back to me, to him I will give the cap."

The foolish men agreed and handed the cap to the sailor. He threw an orange as far as he could, and the two men ran off after it.

"Neither of you is smarter than the other," said the sailor outloud to no one, "or you would not fall for such a simple trick." With that he put on the cap and said, "Cap, cap, cover me up!"

When the two men came back, fighting over the orange, the sailor was nowhere to be seen.

A little further down the road the sailor took the cap off and the world could see him again.

Now the sailor saw two men fighting over a pair of boots.

"This is a most curious town," said the sailor as he walked up to the men. "Tell me why you are fighting."

"We are fighting over this pair of boots," said one man, as he hit the other.

"If it means so much to you, I will gladly give you my boots and I will go barefoot so you may each have boots to wear."

"No, no," said one of the men. "These boots are special. Our father brought them from a wise man in India. In these boots a man may travel seven long leagues of land in the twinkling of an eye. The wearer has only to say, 'Boots, boots, run like the wind,' and he is gone. Our father promised them to whomever of us is the smartest."

"Then I have a plan," said the sailor. "I will take an orange from my pack and throw it as far as I can. To whomever reaches the orange first and brings it back to me, I will give the boots."

The men agreed and handed the boots to the sailor. He took an orange out of his sack and threw it as far as he could. While the men ran off after the orange, the sailor put on the boots and said, "Boots, boots, run like the wind."

In the twinkling of an eye, the sailor was seven leagues away. The two men ran back, quarrelling over the orange, and found him gone.

The sailor was now two leagues out of the town on the other side, so he turned back toward the town square and walked at a normal pace.

On the way back to the square, he saw a large crowd gathered around the steps of the cathedral. The princess had worn out seven more pairs of shoes the night before and the king had decided to make his secret decree public. A town crier was reading it aloud to the people of the town. The sailor heard the promise that whoever solved the mystery could marry the princess, and he decided to give it a try.

The sailor went to the palace of the king, eating an orange out of his sack. When he was let in to see the king, he asked for the king's permission to solve the mystery.

"You are only a simple sailor," said the king. "You are not a wise man nor a magician. How can you solve the mystery of the seven pairs of iron dancing shoes?"

"I ask only that you let me give it a try," replied the sailor.

"Very well," said the king, a little angry. He had not expected common sailors to ask to try! He grinned as he devised a plan to scare the sailor away. "But if you cannot find the answer to this puzzle after three days, I will have you put to death!"

The sailor bowed low before the king and accepted the terms. The king had thought the sailor would not take the risk, but it was too late now. The sailor had to be given a chance to try. The sailor was dressed up in a captain's suit, and seated at the supper table with the royal family. That night, he slept outside the princess's door. As he was falling asleep, the princess opened her door and offered the sailor a drink of water. He was thirsty, so he thanked her and drained the cup. She smiled and went back in, closing her door. When the sailor awoke the next morning, he knew the drink had contained a sleeping potion. As the sun rose, the princess opened the door and walked out, carrying seven pairs of wornout iron dancing shoes.

At the breakfast table, the king asked what the sailor had learned. When the sailor admitted he had learned nothing, the king said, "Two more days, and you die!"

That night the sailor slept inside the door of the princess's bedchamber and he did not take the drink when she offered it. But as he was falling asleep, the princess sprinkled a magic powder on him. When he woke up, he knew he had been tricked again. As the sun rose, Princess Branca walked past him to the door, carrying seven pairs of wornout iron shoes.

At breakfast, the king asked again what the sailor had learned. Again, he replied he had learned nothing. "One more day, and you die!" said the king.

On the third night, the sailor slept on the floor beside the princess's bed, and he would not take the drink she offered, and he kept his eyes open so that she could not sprinkle magic powder over him.

"You have won," said the princess, and she pretended to go to sleep. The sailor also pretended to go to sleep on the carpet. The princess got up and walked toward the door with her seven new pairs of iron dancing shoes. The sailor pulled the magic cap from under his coat and put it on. "Cap, cap," he whispered, "cover me up!"

As the princess went out the door, the sailor followed, but she could not see him. She went down the stairs and out the front door of the royal palace, with the sailor behind her. She got into a beautiful royal coach pulled by six white horses. As the coach sped away, the sailor said to his new boots, "Boots, boots, run like the wind!" and he ran off as fast as the coach and horses were going.

He followed the coach to the seashore, where the princess stepped out of the coach and walked to a pier. Docked at the pier was a fine ship with flags of many colors blowing in the breeze. The princess walked up the gangplank and onto the beautiful ship. The invisible sailor followed. The wind suddenly began to blow very strongly out to sea. The sails of the magic ship filled with wind, and the ship slid silently out from the pier and sailed faster and faster over the waves until it came to the Land of the Giants far out in the Atlantic. There the wind laid low, and the ship glided up to a pier beside the Castle of the King of the Giants.

The princess left the ship and the invisible sailor followed.

At the gate of the castle a huge guard called out, "Who goes there?"

The princess answered, "The Princess of Portugal."

The guard answered, "You may both pass."

As the princess went through the gate, she looked back to see who else the guard was speaking to, but she saw no one.

At the door to the castle, another gigantic guard called out, "Who goes there?"

The princess answered, "The Princess of Portugal."

The guard stepped aside and opened the door for the princess. "You may both pass," he said.

The princess looked back to see who "both" could mean. She saw no one.

At the entryway to the Great Hall of the Giants another enormous guard called out, "Who goes there?"

"The Princess of Portugal."

"You may both pass."

The princess thought these guards must have lost their minds, for she could see no one following her. But this was a magic land, and who could say what was happening?

Fearing that the giants must be able to see him, the sailor hid under a great big chair in the great big Giants' Great Hall. The princess went to the handsome and huge Prince of the Giants, and they joined hands and began to dance as the giants' band played beautiful but very loud music. The sailor watched as the princess danced for an hour, so fast that she wore out a pair of iron shoes. She took off the old shoes and put on a new pair, and she and the handsome giant began to dance again.

Seven hours and seven pairs of shoes later, the sun was about to come up. The ginormous guards entered to announce sunrise, and the princess gathered her wornout shoes to take them home. As she prepared to leave, the guards asked, "Where is your manservant?"

"What manservant?" asked the princess.

"The one who came in with you!" answered the three guards.

"FIND THAT MAN!" roared the prince of the giants. The giants' wise man came into the room with the Giants' Book of Fate, which told everything there is to know about everyone and what their future will be. He opened the book and began to turn the pages, looking for the page that would tell him where the sailor was hiding.

"Boots, boots," said the sailor, "run like the wind." The sailor ran past the wise man, grabbed the Book of Fate, and ran out the door, knocking over all the furniture. The guards and the giants all ran after him, but no one could catch him. The sun was almost coming up when the princess ran onto the magic ship. No one could find the sailor, who was already hiding in the ship with his magic cap, and she couldn't see him either.

The magical wind took the ship back to the mainland of Portugal, and the carriage took the princess back to the palace. The palace was only one league from the Atlantic shore. The magic boots outran the carriage, and when the princess came into her bedchamber, there was the sailor, lying on the carpet, pretending to sleep.

At breakfast, the king asked what the sailor had learned.

The sailor smiled and said, "I saw nothing unusual last night." (And considering what he had seen when he first came to this town, his answer was the truth!)

"Then today you die!" said the king. And soon the king's guards and the royal court had gathered in the courtyard. The royal headsman was standing by with his axe, ready to chop off the sailor's head.

"Do you have any last words?" asked the king.

"I would like to ask the princess a question," said the sailor.

"Ask whatever you like," said the king, impatiently.

"Did My Lady leave her bedchamber last night?" asked the sailor.

"No," said the princess, lying defiantly.

"Did My Lady ride in a carriage to the sea?"

"No!"

"Did My Lady sail in a magic ship to the Land of the Giants?"

"No!"

"Did My Lady dance with the prince of the giants in the Great Hall of the giants' castle?"

"No!"

"And did the guards suspect that someone had followed My Lady?"

"No!"

"And did the wise man of the giants bring forth the Book of Fate to find the manservant who followed you?"

The princess did not answer as quickly this time.

"…no…"The sailor pulled the Book of Fate from inside his coat.

"And is this not that book?"

The princess bowed her head.

"…Yes."

The king shouted with delight that the mystery had been solved. The royal court cheered. The headsman said nothing. The sailor opened the Book of Fate and read aloud:

"And the sailor married the princess, and they lived happily all their days."

The Three Citrons of Love

Alfonso the Fourth-and-a-Half, King of Portugal, had only one son, named Prince Alfonso the Fourth-and-a-Quarter, and the boy was very fond of hunting in the forest. The prince would ride his swiftest horse and carry a lance, hunting deer from horseback. This kind of hunting was called coursing.

As the Prince, who was nicknamed Formoso – The Handsome One, went coursing one day, he met an old woman who looked as if she were starving. The prince never carried silver or gold, but his servants always brought along on their horses large baskets of food to eat at midday deep in the forest. The prince took pity on the old woman and called to his servants to bring the food basket. The servants spread out a cloth upon the grass and served a fine feast of cold leg of mutton and bread and fruits and wine. He asked the old woman to sit down and join him in his midday meal.

The old woman ate and drank her fill, and thanked the kind prince.

"I have nothing valuable to give you in return for your kindness, Prince," she said. "But I do have these three citrons. Please take them!"

Now, citrons are a small fruit like a lime, too sour to eat by themselves. However, hunters often made a kill in the woods and skinned and cooked the meat on the spot. As the meat roasted over the fire, the hunters would squeeze citron juice onto meat to make it more flavorful. Citrons were, in fact, a thoughtful gift to men out on a hunt.

The prince smiled, thinking the gift to be rather worthless, but his heart was touched that this poor woman should want to repay him. He took the three little citrons and bowed low in respect to the old woman.

As the servants packed the basket again, the old woman took her leave of the prince. Her final words were, "When you cut open one of the citrons, do not cut it 'around the waist.' Cut it only long ways, from where the stem has been, back around to where the stem has been."

The prince started to turn and mount his horse. The old woman grabbed his sleeve and added, "Wait! There's more! Always open the citrons only when you are beside a stream or fountain."

Prince Formoso smiled and bowed again, leaping onto his horse to go coursing. He thought all that she said was most strange, but he put the citrons in his hunting bag and went on his way. After he had hunted for an hour without finding any deer, and his servants had gone to the stream to refill the water jars, the prince sat alone on a rock and decided to cut open a citron and smell its pleasant aroma. He took out his skinning knife and one of the citrons. Forgetting what the old woman had said, he cut the citron open around its middle.

Blood poured from the tiny fruit!

Formoso let out a scream and jumped up. The fruit fell to the ground and looked for all the world like a normal citron, but the prince's hands were wet with blood.

The prince dried his hands on a kerchief and took out another citron. He cut it very carefully, as the woman had told him to, longwise, from where the stem had been around to where the stem had been. As he pulled the two halves apart, a small, beautiful young woman stepped out of the citron and grew to full size while standing before him.

"I am very thirsty," she said, for the taste of a citron is sour and makes a person thirsty. "Give me to drink or I will surely die."

The prince had forgotten the second thing the old woman had told him! He was not near a stream or fountain, and had no water to give the lovely young woman.

The beautiful lady saw that the prince had no water. She gave him a very disappointed look. She fell to the ground and died, and withered like a dried fruit until there was nothing left of her but dust, which disappeared into the grass. The prince wept a few tears for his own forgetfulness, and was very sad at the death of this magical maiden.

The prince leapt on his horse, found the servants by the stream, and rode back to the palace. He gave over his horse to his servants and entered his private palace garden by a back gate. He hurried to the fountain in his garden. There he sat down on a marble bench and opened the third citron, cutting from where the stem had been around to where the stem had been.

Out stepped a small, beautiful woman, and she grew to full size before him.

"I am very thirsty," said the maiden from the citron. "Give me to drink or I will surely die."

The prince knelt at the fountain and lifted a handful of cool water, then another, then another. The Citron Maiden drank thirstily, and kissed his hand each time he brought it to her lovely lips.

Formoso and the Citron Maiden spoke for hours, and he fell in love with her. They climbed up onto a tree with low branches and sat there, talking. The prince asked the maiden to wait while he went to do his princely chores, but he advised her to stay in the tree in the garden, so that no one else would see her and ask who she was.

No one would believe the answers she would truthfully give!

While the Prince Formoso was gone and the Citron Maiden sat in the tree, an ugly old woman who worked in the royal kitchen came out to draw water from the prince's fountain. Since the teenaged prince always wanted a snack, a door had been cut from his private garden into the back of the royal kitchen. The ugly old woman entering the garden was evil and she practiced black magic, but she was hired to scrub the floors in the kitchen, for no one knew she was a witch.

She had been forbidden to enter the prince's garden, so she did it every day. She had been forbidden to throw dirty mop water on the prince's flowers, so she did it every day. She had been forbidden to draw clean mop water from the prince's fountain pool, so she did it every day!

Her name was Bruxa Daninha (BROO-shah Dah-NEEN-yah) or Witch Weed, and she threw dirty mop water onto the flowers and walked to the fountain. As the old woman lowered her mop bucket into the water, she looked into the fountain and saw the reflection of the beautiful maiden in the tree above her. She thought it was her own reflection!

"Well, Witch Weed," she said to herself, "this must be a magic pool that makes you so lovely." And she admired herself, turning her head this way and that.

The maiden in the tree saw what the old witch was doing and began to laugh. Being the daughter of a good witch herself, the Citron Maiden immediately recognized this old woman as a bad witch.

Witch Weed looked around to see who was laughing and saw the Citron Maiden in the tree. The old witch knew at once the Citron Maiden was the new-born daughter of the good witch named Bruxa Hamamèlia (BROO-shah Ah-mah-MEH-lee-ah) or Witch Hazel! "Come down, my pretty," said Witch Weed, "and let me brush your lovely hair."

At first the Citron Maiden refused, but the old witch threw magic dust at her, and she came down to the fountain after all. There Witch Weed began to brush the maiden's long hair with the scrub brush she used on dirty floors, asking polite questions about the prince. The Citron Maiden answered, being under the spell of the magic dust. When the bad witch knew all she needed to know, she pulled out a long magical hatpin hidden in her robe. She stuck the hatpin into the poor maiden's head!

But it did not kill her. The hatpin was magic and changed the Citron Maiden into a beautiful white dove, which flew away into the sky.

Witch Weed climbed the tree and sat where the maiden had sat.

Prince Formoso returned and was disgusted to see an old woman (whom he did not recognize as the old maid who scrubbed the floors) sitting where he had left the lovely maiden.

"What has happened?" asked the prince, almost in tears, and feeling a little sick at his stomach.

"I am bewitched, Sweet Prince," said the old woman, trying to talk like the Citron Maiden. "I am lovely some of the time, and ugly the rest."

The prince believed the old woman and took her in. They lived together in the palace, but the witch never got any prettier. Witch Weed had set a wedding day a few weeks in the future. The prince was less enthusiastic than Witch Weed was. One day the prince was walking in the garden, and a beautiful white dove flew down and landed on the tree where the maiden had sat days before. The dove spoke, as if by magic.

"Gardener of my garden," said the bird, "how goes it with the prince and his ugly lady?"

"We are content," answered the prince, still believing the old witch to be the maiden he had loved. He didn't look very content.

The dove flew away.

The next day the prince went walking in the garden at the same hour hoping to see the magic dove again. She flew in and perched on the limb.

"If the prince and his lady are content," said the dove, "then is there no hope for me?"

The dove flew away.

The next day the prince made a bird snare of pretty ribbon to catch the dove. When he set the snare on the limb of the tree, the dove flew in but did not land.

"No snare of ribbon was meant for me," she said, and off she flew.

The next day he set a snare of silver cord.

"No snare of silver was meant for me," said the dove, and off she flew.

The next day he set a snare of tiny golden chain, made from the chains of his old baby necklaces.

"No snare of gold was ever meant for me," the dove said, and off she flew.

The next day he thought of the maiden, and he cut open a citron and left it on the branch where the maiden had once sat. The dove flew in and sat on the branch, and drank the tart juice of the citron. The dove turned and looked at the prince.

"I am very thirsty," said the dove. "Give me to drink or I will surely die."

Then the prince knew who the dove was! He took her in his hands, carried her to the fountain, and gave her a drink from his hand. As he lovingly petted the dove's beautiful head he found a hairpin stuck into her skull. He pulled the pin out, and the dove changed and grew back into the beautiful Citron Maiden.

The prince ordered Witch Weed to be executed for her evil deeds. He made a drum of her skin, and with the long bones of her legs he beat on the drum while everyone danced at the wedding of Prince Formoso and the beautiful Princess Donzela Cidra (Donss-EH-lah SEE-drah), the Citron Maiden.

The Tower of Ill Fortune

Sometimes the brave sailors and explorers from Portugal never returned from their travels, having died in a storm at sea, or been killed by the people of foreign lands. It is no wonder that scary stories were told about the dangers of traveling far from home on land or sea! One man told this story about three brothers living in the mountain range Serra da Estrela (SEH-rah dah Ehs-STREH-lah) northeast of Coimbra, near the border with Spain:

Long ago in the highest mountains of Portugal, there was a young hunter named Tomaz whose father had been to sea, and brought him back a lioness cub from Africa. Soon the cub grew to be a fine young lioness. She hunted with the Tomaz as well as if she were the finest hunting dog.

One day, as Tomaz on horseback, followed by his pet lion, traveled down a narrow pathway in the high mountains, they passed a woman washing clothes in a stream beside the path.

"Greetings, Tiazinha (TEE-ah-SEEN-yah)," he said, addressing her as Auntie. "What are you doing?"

"Washing clothes here," she replied, "and I shall continue to do so all my life. Keep that lion away! Don't let her drool on my clean towels!"

Tomaz called his lion back. Seeing a tower of stone high on the hilltop across the stream, he asked, "Tiazinha, what is the name of that fine tower on the hill?"

"Oh, Sonny," said the old woman, "Don't go there! That is the Tower of Ill Fortune. Whoever goes there…never returns!"

"I shall go there," said Tomaz, foolishly, "and shall return here and find you washing clothes still."

He and his lion crossed the stream. He rode to the tower and found that it had been turned from a watchtower into an inn. He knocked on the door, and an evil-looking old innkeeper opened it. The huntsman asked to purchase lunch.

The old innkeeper said, "Take that horse and that lion and tie them in the stone stable at the end of the courtyard. Mice ate all my rope last winter, so tie them up with…"

Out of his shoulder pouch he pulled a long mysterious braid of human hair.

"…this long mysterious braid of human hair. Tie the lion up good! I don't want her eating my chickens!"

Tomaz, who was very trusting, led his horse to the stable and the lion followed. He tied the braid of hair to the lion's collar and ran the braid through an iron ring set in the stone wall. Then he tied the hair to the horse's halter. The hair didn't look very strong, but he trusted his animals to wait patiently for him to return.

He went to the front door of the tower, opened the heavy wooden door, and went in. Inside the inn, he asked again for lunch. Suddenly the old innkeeper turned mean.

"You'll have to fight me for it!"

They began to fight, knocking over tables and chairs and breaking crockery jugs and plates. The innkeeper was an evil magician and he quickly overpowered the young hunter.

"Come, Horse," called the youth. "Come, Lion! Come and save your master!"

But the magician chanted, "Braid of hair, grow thick! Hold the horse and lion by this trick!"

166

The braid of hair in the stable grew thick until it was as heavy and strong as three-coil rope! The lion and the horse could not break free nor come to save their master.

The magician won the contest, and sprinkled magic powder on the boy. The hunter turned as hard as stone. He stood the stone youth up like a statue in his hall, next to a dozen other turned-to-stone travelers, where animal heads and other trophies hung on the wall. Out of the stone boy's pocket he pulled the bag of gold coins the boy carried…gold cannot be turned to stone by magic…and this is how the innkeeper made his living.

Back at the cabin where they lived, the younger brother of the hunter, whose name was Gill (GHEEL), soon missed his older brother, and went out with his horse and drooling hunting dog to look for him. Soon, on the mountain path, he came to the old woman washing clothes in the stream.

"Greetings, Tiazinha," he said "What are you doing?"

"I already told you!" she said, with irritation. "Washing clothes here, and I shall continue to do so all my life. Oh…keep that drooling dog away from my clean sheets! Don't let him drool on them! Where's your lion?"

"Ah," said Gill. "You saw my older brother Tomaz and his lioness! We do look a lot alike! Did he go to that foreboding tower on the next hill?"

"Oh, Sonny, don't go there," she said. "That's the Tower of Ill Fortune. Whoever goes there never returns."

"I shall go there, and return, and find you washing clothes still."

The younger brother rode up to the inn and knocked on the door. He asked for lunch. The innkeeper gave him a long mysterious braid of hair, and sent the boy to the stable with his horse and dog. There Gill saw the horse and lion of his older brother. He did as the innkeeper told him, patted both horses, the lioness and his dog, and went back into the inn.

"Where is my brother," he asked of the innkeeper, "whose horse and lion are in the stable?"

"You'll have to fight me to find out!"

They began to fight knocking over a table and three chairs and breaking one pottery drinking mug. Gill called out, "Come, Horse! Come, Dog! Come and save your master!"

But the magician said, "Braid of hair, grow thick! Hold the horse and dog by this trick!"

The hair braid in the stable grew so thick and heavy that the animals could not go to the aid of their master. Soon the second brother was cold as stone and standing like a statue in the trophy hall next to his brother and under a lot of animal heads on the wall. The innkeeper reached into the middle brother's stone pocket and pulled out a bag of silver coins. Silver cannot be turned to stone by magic. This is, after all, how the innkeeper made his living.

Not long afterwards, back at their cabin in the woods, the youngest brother, whose name was Jaime (ZHAH-ee-meh) was getting really hungry for lunch. He was a teenager and therefore had no idea how to cook a meal by himself. He missed his two older brothers and set out riding on his pony, carrying his kitty cat to find where they had gone. Sooner than you might expect, he came to the woman at the stream washing clothes.

"Greetings, Tiazinha. What are you doing?"

"How many times do I have to tell you?" she yelled. "Washing clothes here, and I shall continue to do so all my life. And keep that…Oh! Your lion has shrunk. You've got to wash lions in cold water or they shrink! Everyone knows that!"

"Was my brother here with his lioness? My other brother with his dog?" The old woman nodded to both questions. "Did they go to that tower on yonder hill?"

"Oh, Sonny, don't go there! That is the Tower of Ill Fortune. Whoever goes there never returns."

"I shall go there and return, and find you here washing clothes still."

Quicker than you can say, "Tower of Ill Fortune" three times, the youngest brother knocked on the door of the inn. He asked for a lunch…a really big lunch. He was fourteen.

"Here," said the evil innkeeper, "Take this long mysterious braid of human hair…and I hope you ain't got any more brothers because I'm running out of braids…and tie up your puny little pony and your pathetic little puss-cat in the stable."

Jaime led his pony, and carried his kitty, to the stable. As he walked, he asked some very good questions of himself.

"Whose hair is this anyway?" he asked himself out loud. "And did they donate it voluntarily?"

In the stable he saw the lion and horse of Tomaz, and the horse and dog of Gill. They were tied with very thick hair braids. He decided something was wrong. He gave his horse hay and set his cat loose to find mice. He took out his hunting knife and cut his braid of hair into small pieces. Then he cut loose the horses, the dog…the lion looked mad and hungry so left her tied…and he also cut the fatter hair braids into small pieces. He looked for a trash receptacle, but he couldn't find one, so he politely put all the pieces into his shoulder pouch, and went back into the inn to find a trash can.

"Where are my brothers?" he asked.

"You'll have to fight me to find out!" was the answer.

They began to fight. The youngest brother bumped one table, knocked over one chair and broke…into a sweat. The magician-innkeeper began to win.

"Come, horses! Come, Dog! Come, Cat! Come and save your masters!"

"Braid of hair," chanted the innkeeper, "grow thick…"

"This stuff?" asked Jaime, pulling all the cut up hair out of his shoulder pouch. He quickly stuffed the hair into the innkeeper's wide-open mouth.

As the third braid grew thick, the evil innkeeper swelled up like a toad on a hot summer day and he burst into a thousand bloody... and very hairy...pieces.

The hair braid on the lion melted like wax in a hot fire. The horses, the lion, the dog, and the cat came from the stable. The evil spells on the brothers melted away, and the young men came down to meet their youngest brother. The other people turned to stone woke up and asked what day it was. The animal heads on the wall did not change. Everyone searched among the burst innkeeper pieces and found their own bag of coins, and started for home.

The three brothers raided the kitchen and found cold meat and cheese and fresh bread to eat. They rode out of the courtyard of the inn and back to the woman washing clothes in the stream.

"Are you washing still?" they called out, laughing.

"If I want to eat," she said, angrily.

The boys laughed again. They told her to give up washing and go to the tower, and there to clean up the horrible mess and take up the career of innkeeper. And to this day she keeps that inn, in the highest mountain road in Portugal, not too far from the Spanish border, and if you stop there and ask for lunch, while you're eating, she'll wash your shirt and tell you this story.

On the Atlantic Shore of Spain

On the southwestern coast of Spain there is a salty river, the Rio Saltés that empties into the Atlantic. Up that salty river, past a marsh, lies the confluence of two rivers. One is the Río Odiel (REE-oh Oh-thee-EHL), the river on which the large city of Huelva (WELL-vah) is located. The other river is the Tinto (REE-oh TEEN-toh), and on it are the towns of Moguer (Moh-GHEHR) and Palos (PAH-lohss.) Palos was sometimes called Palos de Moguer because it was close to the larger town named Moguer. Palos de Moguer is the protected, inland port from which Columbus' three ships had sailed on August 3, 1492. Being a short distance upriver, the port allowed ships to rest in calm water, away from the stormy North Atlantic Ocean. Most of the sailors on Columbus's three ships had come from the towns along these rivers, and from across southern Spain. The men's families waited in their homes on this historic night, worrying about their menfolk who were far away at sea. Their menfolk had been gone more than two months.

As Columbus' crews slept silently on their three ships, their families were waking up just at dawn on the morning of October 13, 1492. No one knew it at the time, but the entire world was about to change from small nations and kingdoms to large empires and alliances reaching around the globe. The last night of the Late Middle Ages was ending, and from the morning of October 13, 1492, on, historians call the time we live in the Modern Age. Over the next five hundred years the Earth would go from creaking wooden sailing ships to fast automobiles, jet planes and rocket-launched trips to the Moon and from hand-copied books to printed books to graphic novels to e-readers!

The sun was beginning to rise over the town of Palos de Moguer where the wives and sisters and daughters and young sons of the Pinzón families...the men who owned two of Columbus' ships...were awaiting their menfolk's return. The families were up and the breakfasts were cooking on the fires. While she stirred the pot, one grandmother told the young children their favorite fairy tale.

Black and Yellow

Once it was that there was a little hill in the southern mountains of Spain that looked very much like the little loaf of fresh bread your grandmother just took out of the oven – it was called El Panecillo (Ehl pah-neh-SEEL-yoh, a small round loaf of bread a bit bigger than a dinner roll) but, of course, this Panecillo was as big as a hill. On either side of this El Panecillo there was a village.

To the east of the hill was a little village where everyone dressed all in yellow from their caps to their shoes, all in yellow. Their banner was a little yellow flag, and their gardens were full of yellow flowers. The people of the town were always at play. They never did any work at all; every day was a holiday and every meal was a picnic. Everyone laughed and sang and danced and played their guitars. But something was missing from their lives. They weren't sure what. But if you asked them if they were happy playing all the time, they would answer, "We cannot know, for we are always partying. We have nothing to compare it to."

On the west side of the little round mountain was another village, where everyone dressed all in black -   from their hoods to their boots, all in black. Their flag was a little black banner, and their pots and their kettles and their hinges and door handles were all of the finest, shiniest black iron. The people of the town were always at work. They never played at all; every day was a workday. The men were always sawing or hammering; the women were always working in the homes, cooking, cleaning, sweeping the floors. If the floors were clean they swept the paths to their front stoops. If the paths were clean they went out and swept the cobblestone streets. Everyone was solemn and silent and serious, and very, very hard at work. But if you asked them if they were happy, they would say, "We cannot know, for we are always working. We have nothing to compare it to."

One day a wise man got tired of giving people good advice and teaching wiggly little children to be wise. He decided to go on a vacation. He went walking down the road because he did not own a horse, and besides, walking was good for you. He walked away from the town where he was the official Wise Man, and was walking along the winding road through the mountains enjoying the fresh air. Fresh air is good for you.

He came to the little village where everyone dressed all in yellow. He saw them laughing and singing and dancing, and playing their guitars. He said to himself, "Ah, it must be a *día de fiesta* (Dee-ah deh Fee-EHSS-tah, a holiday) Because he was wise and valued wisdom above all else, he wanted to ask the partying people a question. It took a long time to quiet the people so they could hear him in the village square, or plaza. Finally he asked them if they were happy. They said, "We cannot know, for we are always playing. We have nothing to compare it to."

The people dressed in yellow went back to singing, dancing and playing their guitars.

The wise man was troubled by their answer, but he was on vacation and decided not to give them any advice on how to be happy. He went on and walked around the little round mountain until he came to the village where everyone was dressed all in black. He saw them gardening and cleaning and chopping wood and polishing the ironwork grills on the windows of their houses. Everyone was solemn, silent, and serious. The wise man wanted to learn if these people were happy. He called for their attention and everyone got quiet, put down their hammers and brooms, and lined up in an orderly row in front of the wise man, just as they did for the schoolteacher or the priest. When the wise man asked if they were happy, they said, "We cannot know, for we are always working. We have nothing to compare it to."

Then the wise man knew he must do something very wise to help the people in these two villages find happiness. The wise man knew many things, and he also knew all the right magic words. I am sorry to say that in the many centuries that have passed since this story happened, most of the magic in the world has melted in the morning sun and floated away on the mist, leaving behind only wisdom. But this was long ago, and the wise man knew powerful magic words. He made his plan.

The wise man stood in the plaza of the village where everyone was dressed all in black.

"*Señores* (Sehn-YOHR-ehs) and *señoras* (sehn-YOHR-ahs), Ladies and Gentlemen, let me have your attention, please. Tomorrow morning I will be on the top of El Panecillo, and if you will meet me there, we will do some work together!"

All the people nodded and said, "It is good. We would like to do some new work for a change. Tomorrow, in the morning, we will be there."

Then the wise man went back around the little mountain to the plaza of the village where everyone was dressed all in yellow. He called to them…he called to them…he yelled "BE QUIET FOR A MOMENT!" and they got quiet.

"Señores and señoras, let me have your attention, please. Tomorrow morning I will be on top of El Panecillo, and if you will meet me there we will have a party together."

All the people cheered and laughed and sang and danced and played their guitars. The ones who weren't cheering or singing said, "It is good. We would like to have a party on a mountaintop. Tomorrow, in the morning, we will be there."

As the sun rose over the mountains of southern Spain and the first beam of sunlight struck the little round mountain, there sat the wise man with his legs crossed and his arms folded. Up the eastern side of the mountain came the people all dressed in yellow, laughing and singing and dancing, and carrying picnic baskets and guitars. Up the western side of the mountain came the people all dressed in black, carrying axes and hammers and gardening tools for whatever kind of civic work might be required on a mountaintop.

When the people all dressed in yellow saw the people all dressed in black, they began to shout insults at each other and shake their fists in the air.

The people dressed in black shook their fingers at the other villagers and shouted, "Lazy! Loafers! Worthless ones! Why don't you keep your room clean? Why don't you get better grades like your older sister?"

The people dressed in yellow thumbed their noses at the other villagers and shouted, "Home Bodies! Party Poopers! Stuck-in-the-muds! People in yellow just want to have fun!"

Pretty soon all the people were quarreling and fighting and poking each other in the nose. The wise man unfolded his arms, raised his hands high, and said the most powerful magic word he knew.

Suddenly, no one was dressed all in yellow, and no one was dressed all in black.

Now everyone was dressed the same: one stripe of yellow, one stripe of black, one stripe of yellow, one stripe of black. And now no one wanted to work all the time and no one wanted to play all the time. Now they all agreed on what was the wise thing to do.

When the sun was high and yellow in the sky, the people went out to work in their gardens or in the fields, but they laughed and talked as they worked, and they sang going to and from the fields. When the womenfolk brought lunch to the menfolk in the fields they made a picnic of it.

When night fell, and the sky was black and the streets were dark with shadows, the people went into their houses or into the plaza and danced and played their guitars around the yellow light of candles and lanterns.

Now the people were happy, for they had both work and play to give variety to their days, and could compare the two.

A very odd thing happened. As the years rolled by and turned into centuries, the magic in the world melted in the morning sun and floated away in the mist. As the magic evaporated, these people dressed in black-and-yellow grew smaller and smaller, until they were no bigger than your thumbnail. They left their villages and moved into little round homes like the little round mountain, about the size of an overturned bucket.

When the sun is high and yellow in the sky these people come out with the morning sun and float into the air like the morning mist. They fly to the fields and gather harvest from the flowers. When the sky is black with night, they fly back to their little round house, bringing home the pollen and nectar they have harvested. They sing and dance around their little house, and they play on tiny guitars.

These little people are the bees. There were no bees in the world until the wise man said that magic word.

And I know the story to be true, because my grandfather told it to me.

The Young Lovers of Teruel

One of the older girls, a daughter of one Columbus' captains, told another story as the breakfast finished cooking. It is a very sad love story, and she told it to her younger sisters:

It happened that there were, in the village of Teruel (Tehr-WELL) in the Kingdom of Aragón (Ah-rah-GOHN), two children, a boy and a girl, whose families' mansions were side by side. Both families were noble, but one family still had all their wealth, while the other family had fallen on hard times, as sometimes happened to noble families in the olden days. The little girl's family was very rich, but the little boy's family was quite poor, in spite of the large house in which they lived. The children played together and became great friends, and since both children were of noble birth, their families approved of their friendship.

As the years passed the friendship turned to love, and the poor young hidalgo (ee-DAHL-goh, a nobleman), named Diego asked the lovely doncella (dohn-SELL-yah, young lady) named Isabel for her hand in marriage. While Isabel freely agreed, being very much in love with Diego, her father refused to give his permission because Diego's family was so poor.

Diego protested that keeping them apart would break their hearts, but the girl's father would not change his mind. All seemed lost for the young lovers from Teruel. At last, after Isabel begged her father to think it over, he agreed that if Diego would go out into the world and earn a fortune in six years time, he would give his permission for the two to marry.

Diego asked the nobleman to promise him he would not give his daughter's hand in marriage to anyone else for six years, to give Diego a chance to earn a fortune and win his beloved's hand. The girl's father agreed.

Young Diego could think of only one way to win a fortune in so short a time. There was a great war being fought in the Near East, over who would control the Biblical city of Jerusalem which was sacred to the Jewish people, the Muslims, and the Christians. It was the year 1211, and Diego set out on foot for Italy, from which armies going to the Holy Land had set sail.

In the years that followed, Diego served as a squire…a knight's assistant…and eventually became a knight himself. He was made a captain of the army, then a commander. Every day he thought only of his beloved Isabel, and the memory of her made him ride faster and work harder than any of the other knights. Finally, Diego had horses, armor, and a chest of silver and gold coins for his service to kings. It was time to return to Aragón, to the city of Teruel, and claim his beloved. The journey home was long, and his pack mules moved slowly. Years had passed, and Diego's time was running out. Finally it was one day before the sixth anniversary of his departure, and he was not yet home. He struggled over the dirt roads, as fast as he was able to go, as the sun rose on the last day of Isabel's father's promise.

Diego was still one day's journey from Teruel!

Back at the family's mansion, Isabel's father had counted the days very carefully and knew that the time for keeping his promise was nearly at an end. He went into the bedchamber of his daughter and told her what day it was. He also reminded her that in all the six years she had never received any news of Diego (who had been too far away and in circumstances too difficult to write a letter or send a message.) He reminded her that, for all they knew, Diego might have died years ago in a war in a faraway land.

Isabel wept quietly. She feared that her father spoke the truth that, in fact, her Diego was probably among the dead.

Her father told Isabel that another nobleman, Don Azagra (Ah-SAH-grah) by name, had recently asked for her hand in marriage, and that he had given his permission, provided the six-year promise had come to an end. Isabel sadly agreed that when the six years were up, she would marry Azagra, who was wealthy and handsome.

When the anniversary day came and the six years had ended, the wedding feast was held in the mansion of Don Azagra. Not far away, along the dusty road, Diego was coming closer one day too late. The wedding took place and the families embraced each other and rejoiced. The wedding guests ate and drank and sang and danced. But Isabel was sad, and asked her husband to understand why she wanted to sleep alone that night in a quiet room. Don Azagra was a kind man and loved Doña Isabel very much, so he agreed to stay and entertain the guests while she went upstairs to sleep in a quiet bedchamber.

In the privacy of her room, Isabel sat by the fire and sang softly to herself, happy to be married to so kind a man, but sad at the loss of her beloved Diego. Just at that moment, like the dreams she had been having for six years and a day, Diego stepped into her

bedchamber. He had arrived at Teruel, one day late, and gone straight to the mansion of Isabel's family where the servants, who did not recognize him, told him of the wedding at the mansion of Don Azagra. Climbing the vines on the columns of the porch, Diego entered the room the last steps of a journey of a thousand leagues.

Doña Isabel gasped at the sight of him older, bearded, greying, and dirty from the road. She did not recognize him! He spoke and she almost fainted.

Diego fell to his knees and told her of the long journey, of the years on the path of adventure and adversity, of his inability to send word home, of the hundred times he had risked his life as a knight to earn a fortune for the two of them to live on throughout their life together. He told of coming home, of visiting her mansion without even going to his own home, of learning of the wedding from the servants, and of passing unrecognized through the wedding guests to climb to her chamber.

He begged her for one kiss, one last kiss.

She wept and held his hand in hers. She was married now, to an honorable man, and she would not break the promises she had made in the wedding ceremony only hours before. Isabel loved Diego more than she loved her own life, but she had made vows before God in the wedding ceremony, and her duty now was to kind Don Azagra. If Diego had come only one day earlier, she would have greeted him not with one kiss, but with one thousand kisses. Now they both knew it was too late.

Diego, on his knees before her and still holding her hand, bowed his head in sorrow. He clutched at his heart with his other hand and fell at her feet, dead of a broken heart. Diego, the son of the nobleman Don García (Gahr-SEE-ah), was no more.

Isabel wept bitterly and released his hand from hers, laying it across his chest on the dusty tabard with its bright red cross. She knelt beside him, folded her hands, and began to pray for his soul. Much later, Don Azagra came to her door to see if she were well; one of the servants had heard her crying. She greeted him and told him that she had had a nightmare. She said she had dreamed that Don Diego came back from the crusades and wanted one last kiss. She said she had dreamed that she refused him, and his heart broke and he fell dead at her feet. She asked what her new husband thought she should have done had this happened for real, instead of in a dream.

Knowing of his new bride's love for Don Diego, and being a kind man, Don Azagra smiled. He said if it had happened in real life he would have understood, and she would have been permitted to give her former lover one last kiss. At this, Doña Isabel burst into tears. She told Don Azagra it had not been a dream. Don Diego lay dead in her bedchamber.

Sadly, Don Azagra and a trusted servant lifted the body of Don Diego and carried it to the front door of Don García's mansion. They laid the body down carefully, so it looked as if Don Diego, tired and worn out from the long journey home, had died of relief just as he was about to enter his own home. The treasure chest he had brought with him was laid beside him. The treasure would make his poor family wealthy once more. He had been a good son and a dear friend.

The funeral was held the following day, and all the people of Teruel went to the burial in the chapel nearby. Don Azagra and Doña Isabel went also, dressed in the black clothing of mourning. Just before the casket was to be closed and pushed into a vault, Doña Isabel stepped forward and bent over the body of her former childhood sweetheart. She spoke softly to the body, saying that she had brought him the one last kiss he had requested the night before. She kissed Don Diego goodbye and laid her head on the chest of the man who was to have been her husband.

When Doña Isabel did not stand after a long while, Don Azagra rushed forward to her.

Doña Isabel had died, her own heart broken, resting her head on the chest of Don Diego. They were buried side by side in stone tombs, in their village in Aragón, a town that has never forgotten the young lovers from Teruel.

The two younger daughters of one of Columbus' ship captains were shedding a tear or two, sad at the end of the story of the ill-fated young lovers Isabel and Diego. The oldest daughter quickly began to tell a silly story to cheer her sisters up again:

Bastianito

Some people are so silly! And this is the story of a family that was full of them. In the town just over the mountain from ours, there lived a foolish man named Sebastián (Seh-bahst-YAHN) with his foolish wife Bobita (Boh-BEE-tah). They had a daughter named Carmen, who was lovely but a little silly.

A local farm boy asked Carmen for her hand in marriage and she accepted. So the boy went to Don Sebastián and asked for his permission to marry the girl. When Don Sebastián and Bobita had given permission, a great wedding feast was planned. One thing they wanted to have was enough good wine to drink at the feast, for the water in the village well was full of toads and no good to drink. Sebastián bought three barrels of good red wine, and had them rolled into the cellar under the house. The whole village, including many people who weren't even invited, gathered for the wedding feast, and everyone sat down to eat and drink before the wedding ceremony. Soon everyone had drunk their wine and there was no more in the pitchers to serve the guests. Carmen wanted to show what a good wife she was going to be to José (Hoh-SEH), the farm boy, so she volunteered to go to the basement and get more wine. She took the pitchers and walked down the spiral stone staircase to the basement.

She put the first pitcher under the spigot set into the barrel and turned it open. The wine began to flow out of the barrel through the spigot and into the pitcher. As she waited for the pitcher to fill, Carmen did what she usually did when she was supposed to be doing a chore…she began to daydream.

"When this pitcher is full, I will go upstairs," she thought, "and when the meal is over, I will be married. When the ceremony is over, José and I will move to a farmhouse and set up housekeeping, and soon I'll have a fine baby son and we will name him Bastianito, 'Little Sebastián,' after my dear father. When he grows up he will be a soldier and go off to war. But if he should die, oh, how I would cry!"

At the thought of little Bastianito, who wasn't even born yet, dying in a battle, Carmen began to cry and cry.

The wine pitcher was full, and the wine kept flowing out of the barrel. The wine overflowed the pitcher and ran onto the basement floor. Carmen cried and cried for poor Bastianito, who had died in a battle and hadn't been born yet!

After a while, the guests were getting thirsty and Bobita said, "I'll go down and see what's keeping our daughter." She went down the spiral stone staircase into the cellar. There was Carmen, crying and crying, with the wine up to her ankles on the cellar floor.

"Why are you crying?" asked Bobita.

"I daydreamed I was married and had a son named Bastianito. He became a soldier and he died in a battle!" said Carmen.

"Oh, my poor grandson, already killed in a battle," moaned Bobita, "and him not even born yet!" She began to cry and cry, and the wine kept pouring out of the barrel onto the floor of the cellar.

After a while, the guests at the feast were getting really thirsty, so Don Sebastián said, "I'll go down and see what's keeping my wife and daughter."

Down the spiral stone staircase he went into the cellar. There stood Bobita and Carmen, crying and crying, with the wine up to their calves on the cellar floor.

"Why on earth are you crying?" asked Don Sebastián.

Bobita said, "Carmen daydreamed she was married and had a son named Bastianito. He became a soldier and was killed in a battle! Poor little fellow! He wasn't even born yet!"

"Oh, my poor namesake, killed in a battle," gasped Don Sebastián, "and him not even born yet!" He, too, began to cry and cry, and the wine kept pouring out of the barrel onto the floor of the cellar.

After a while, the guests at the feast upstairs were as dry as wheat chaff, and the groom said, "I'll go down and see what's keeping my bride-to-be, and my mother-in-law-to-be, and my father-in-law-to-be."

Down he went, down the spiral stone staircase into the cellar, where he stepped into a pool of red wine. There stood Carmen, Bobita, and Don Sebastián, crying and crying.

"Why on earth are all of you crying?" asked José.

Don Sebastián said, "Carmen dreamed you and she were married, and you had a son named Bastianito. He became a soldier and died in a battle!"

José waded through the wine, which came up to his knees on the cellar floor, and turned off the spigot in the barrel. The wine stopped pouring out.

"You three are such sillies!" he shouted over sound of crying and wine spilling. "I cannot marry your daughter," he said to Don Sebastián and Bobita. "I will go out into the world and seek my fortune. I would not come back here unless I found three people sillier than you, which is not very likely!"

With that, José turned around in the wine and waded back to the stairs. His shoes squished as he climbed back up to the feast.

"Where's the wine?" called the guests, hoarse from thirst.

"It's in the cellar," said José. "Go swim in it!"

As he left the house, he could hear the guests laughing and splashing in the cellar, swimming in the wine, and trying to console the foolish family who were crying over their poor dead grandson who hadn't been born yet.

José went to his house and packed all his belongings in a spare linen handkerchief. Everything fit nicely, because all he owned was a spare linen handkerchief. He also put in a loaf of bread and a flask of wine that his mother and father gave him. He set out at once to seek his fortune, with his belongings tied in a bundle on a stick.

Off he went down the road. He came to the village well, which was full of toads. Beside the well was a man with a water jar full of toads and a copper sieve all full of holes. He was lowering the sieve into the well, bringing it up, and pouring the water into the jar. But most the water ran out by the time he got the sieve to the top of the well, and just about all that went into the jar was an occasional toad.

"What are you doing, Tío?" asked Giuseppe, even though the man wasn't really his uncle.

"Filling my jar with this sieve," he answered. "But it is taking me a great long while."

"No, Tío," said José, "you don't get water in a sieve. You get water in a bucket."

With that, José went to a neighboring house and borrowed a bucket. Soon the man's water jar was full and all the toads swam out over the rim and hopped away.

The man thanked José, and José walked away thinking, "Well, there's one man sillier than my in-laws-to-have-been!"

José walked a little further. This was a whole village of people who were not too bright, and he soon came upon a man sitting in a tree with his stockings on, jumping to the ground near a pair of leather boots.

"What are you doing, Tío?" asked José.

"Can't you see that I'm trying to put on my new boots?" asked the man as he climbed back up the tree, took aim, and jumped again, missing the boots entirely. "I've been at this a great long while, but I still can't get them on."

"No, Tío," said José, "you don't put on boots that way. You do it like this."

With that, José took off his own boots and set them aside, and pulled on the man's leather boots one at a time to show him how. When he had the other man's boots on he said, "See?"

"Say," said the silly man, "that looks easy!" He took José's boots and put them on one at a time, just as José had done.

"Say," said the silly man, looking down at José's boots, "these boots don't fit me at all."

After José got the man's boots off, and took his own boots off the man's feet, and put his own boots back on himself, which took quite a while in itself, the man thanked José and put on his own new boots. José went away thinking, "Well, that's another man sillier than my in-laws-to-have-been!"

José went on a little further, but remember, this was an entire community of knot heads. He soon came to a wedding party just outside the gate to the churchyard. There he saw a groom on foot and his bride-to-be riding a fine white horse. The bride was so tall in the saddle of the great war horse that she could not ride under the crosspiece above the gate into the churchyard. Everyone was standing around, scratching their heads.

"What are you doing, Primos?" asked José, even though these silly people were not actually his cousins.

"We are supposed to be married," said the groom, "but we can't get into the church. My bride-to-be can't ride under the crosspiece over the gate. She's too tall."

"Cut the horse's legs off shorter," suggested one wedding guest.

"No, no," said another guest, "cut the bride's head off. She'll fit if you just cut her head off!"

"This isn't much of a wedding, anyway," said another guest. "I hear there is a wedding across town where they filled the whole cellar with wine! I'd go there instead, only I've never been across town before!"

"No, No, Primos," said José, "you don't cut off the horse's legs or the bride's head."

José walked up to the horse, and turned and said to the groom-to-be, "Let me kiss the bride now, I can't stay for the whole wedding."

When the girl bent over to kiss José, he slapped the horse's rump and the horse ran through the gate before the bride could sit back up. Everyone ran through the gate and into the church, cheering. The groom thanked José, and shook his hand for quite a while. José went away thinking, "Maybe I didn't have it so bad after all."

With that, he took all his worldly possessions and his loaf of bread and his flask of wine, and went back to the house of his bride-to-be. There he found Don Sebastián chiseling a marble gravestone that said 'Bastianito' on it, just in case José came back, and married Carmen, and they had a son named Bastianito, and he became a soldier and was killed in a battle.

"Well, I'm back," said José to Carmen, who came out to greet him all dressed in black to mourn her poor son who had died in battle before he had even had a chance to be born.

They were married and had a fine son whom they named

Bastianito. He became a government employee, so he was never troubled with having to work or think a difficult thought in his life. And as for that marble tombstone, well, he just used it as a paperweight until his desk fell through the floor into the cellar of the city hall where all the wine barrels were stored.

Everyone in that village was so *tonto* [dumb] that I moved out of that village, with all my belongings bundled up in my spare linen handkerchief, and came here to tell you the story of Bastianito.

The Witch of Amboto

The story behind this story: The Basque (pronounced like the English word bask) people are a unique European national and ethnic group who speak an ancient language unrelated to any other language on earth. They must have lived in Europe before anyone else arrived! Where they live in France and Spain is called Euskal Herria or Basque Country. They call themselves *euskal herritarrak* or "natives of the Basque Country," and their language is called Euskara (in English: Basque.) The words and phrases in Basque in this legend are just used like salt and pepper to flavor the story. See if you can learn their meaning just by reading the story! The meanings of the words are listed after the story, and in the Glossary at the end of this book. This is an ancient story from the Euskal Herria of northeastern Spain in the 1400's. The story tells about the tiny village of Amboto, located about six miles due south of Durango in the Spanish province of Biscaya. The village of Anboto (in Basque) is pronounced Amboto in Spanish, and The Witch of Amboto is not who you think she is!

The Basque Country of northeastern Spain is on the Bay of Biscay, and many Basques sailed ships in the Atlantic. A young serving boy in the Pinzón family was a Basque from far northern Spain. He thrilled the captain's young daughters with a scary story from his native region far to the north!

Anbotoko Sorgina

The Witch of Amboto, retold here in English, Spanish and Euskara.

In the Basque Country of northern Spain and southwestern France, there are many dark legends. The most frightening is a tale of the Anbotoko Sorgina...the Witch of Amboto.

Between the Ebro River in Spain and the Garonne River in France is Vasconia, the domain of the Basques. The Basques are an ancient people whose language is not related to any other language in Europe or the Middle East; the Basques must have lived in the mountains and caves for an unimaginably long time. Their villages are scattered between high ridges and peaks, hidden in forested valleys. In the shadows of the limestone ridge known as Alluitz-Anboto lies the small Basque village of Amboto where, sometime in the 1300's, an act of evil witchcraft took place.

On the seventh night of the week, at the seventh hour, as the bells in the church steeple were ringing seven, a cold wind blew down off the mountain, clouds rolled over the valley, and a high cruel laugh could be heard in the sky above the village of Amboto. Those who dared look up said they saw a witch woman flying over the village and fields. She was dressed all in red, as red as blood, and under her dress she wore six red petticoats, which are called *basquiñas* in Spanish because only Basque women wore them in the Middle Ages.

This Witch Dressed in Red flew down and around the village,

and out over the fields of wheat. Above seven different fields of wheat she dropped one of her basquiñas and it floated down and draped itself over the stalks. When seven petticoats had been dropped, she flew back high up the mountain and disappeared in the dark clouds.

When the sun rose on Sunday morning, seven families going to church passed their fields and found all the stalks dry and the ears of wheat…the part you eat…withered as if there had been a drought for many months. Seven families lost their year's income that day. The mayor of Amboto called a town meeting at the oak tree in the middle of the village, where local officials took their oaths of office. A large crowd…well…large for Amboto, gathered around him.

"As mayor of the town, I pledge seven coins of silver to anyone who can kill the Red Witch!" he shouted. Everyone cheered. All the young men went home and restrung their bows, sharpened their arrows and glued fletching on their arrows that was coming loose with age. Many young archers hid in their families' fields that night.

Nothing happened.

By sunset the following seventh day, *larunbatean* in Basque, no one was waiting in the fields anymore. At the seventh hour, as the bell in the church tower rang seven times, the dark clouds rolled over the valley and the high, cackling laugh was heard. Again the Red Witch flew down over the valley. Seven petticoats she dropped on seven fields. Seven families awoke to find their crops dried out, ruined. The Anbotoko alkatea, the mayor of Amboto, called another meeting.

"I pledge seven coins of gold to whoever can kill the gorria sorgina! The Red Witch must die!" This time the young men waited until the next larunbatean before they went to the wheat fields to wait for the Red Witch. Again, at the seventh hour, as the bell tolled seven, the witch dressed in red flew down off the mountain. She dropped her seven red basquiñas on seven more fields. Several young men shot an arrow toward her, but she flew too high, she flew too fast, she got away. The next day, seven fields were parched and desiccated. And in a field where a young man had been hiding and one of the seven red basquiñas fell, the young man was found dead, withered, dried up like a mummy buried in a cave for a century.

After the sad funerals for the brave dead boys, the alkatea called another meeting at the oak tree in the middle of town. "I pledge…to the youth who kills the gorria sorgina…with her red petticoats…" He thought of the most precious thing he owned. "…the hand of my daughter in marriage!"

People first gasped, then cheered. The unmarried boys cheered loudest, because the alkatea's daughter was beautiful and well-loved throughout the village. One boy was not at all pleased, and did not cheer. He had loved the alkatea's daughter since childhood and had asked her to marry him. He made his plans very carefully for the next larunbatean.

As the bell in the church tower rang five in the evening, the boyfriend of the alkatea's daughter readied his bow and quiver of arrows. He walked toward his family's field and sat down in the tall wheat out of sight. At once he began to crawl through the field with his bow and quiver on his back. He came to a grove of trees and stood up where no other town boy could see that he had left his family's field.

He stood up and began to run up the side of the mountain of Amboto on a hunting trail. If he could get high enough uphill, he would be the first to see the evil Red Witch, the closest to her before she flew out over the valley, the one with the best chance of killing her.

He loved the alkatea's daughter and would risk anything to win her hand in marriage. His love would triumph!

Halfway up the mountain, where the fields of gari were small and far between, he became weary. He realized that in his haste to get a head start on the other boys, he had forgotten to bring along a gourd of drinking water. He was very thirsty. He walked around the edge of a cliff, looking for a stream.

Suddenly he heard a high, cackling laugh nearby. He dropped low among the stalks of gari in the nearest field. He looked all around him. In the limestone rock face of the cliff he saw a pale light. He crept toward the light.

He came to the mouth of a cave. Peering around the edge of the cave mouth, he saw two women seated by a fire. One was the evil Witch Dressed in Red. The other was the good Witch Dressed in White! He had heard of her all his life! She was Mari, the Anbotoko Sorgina…the Good Witch of Amboto!

"Sister," said the zuri sorgina, the White Witch, "Why do you curse the *eremuan*…the fields…of the people of Amboto?"

"Ah…Sister!" said the gorria sorgina. "I have done a foolish thing. My wheat fields were poor and stunted, not strong and tall like everyone else's fields of gari! I wanted my little wheat eremuan to be the best, and my ears of gari to bring the best price! So I made a contract with the devil."

" 'Your gari will be the best'," the devil said, 'When everyone's else's gari is dead!"

The Red Witch shook her head sadly. "But what does it profit me to have all the gold in the world if I lose my immortal soul?"

"My people will starve if all the gari dies on the stalk!" said the Good Witch of Amboto. "Is there nothing anyone can do to break this evil contract you foolishly made with the devil?"

"If only a person who is pure of heart would rub his arrow with seven ears of gari…" the gorria sorgina said sadly, "…and when the bell rings seven, pull the bowstring back to touch his heart, with that arrow I could be killed. My soul would be free of the contract with the devil."

The Red Witch sighed. "But no one knows," she said.

"No one knows," the White Witch said. She turned and looked straight into the eyes of the boy hidden in the darkness! She winked!

"I know!" he whispered. He turned and ran as fast as he could back to the nearest eremuan. He knelt and broke off seven ears of gari. He rubbed his sharpest arrow with the ears of wheat. The bell in the valley below began to ring.

One… He notched his arrow to the bowstring.

Two…The wind began to blow.

Three…the Red Witch cackled in the cave.

Four…The dark clouds rolled down the hillside and started out over the valley.

Five…The boy pulled the bowstring back as far as he could. This arrow would fly farther and faster than any he had every shot before.

Six…Out of the cave came the Red Witch flying only tree-top high over the boy. It would be an easy shot!

Seven…The boy touched the bowstring, pulled back as far as he could pull it, to his heart…and let the arrow fly!

Lightning flashed. Thunder rolled. Close above him he heard a scream. A warm droplet hit his cheek. It was not rain.

It was blood.Out across the valley thousands of droplets of blood fell like a warm spring rain. In every eremuan where a drop of blood hit the earth…

…a little red flower grew.

   …a little red poppy grew.

      …a little red poppy grew among the gari.

When the sun rose the next morning, the stalks of gari were tall and ripe with long ears bending in the wind. Good gari…good grain…good flour…good bread!

The boy and the alkatea's daughter were wed. The village celebrated. And ever since, when the gari is planted in any eremuan near Amboto, each family plants poppies between the rows in the field in memory of the night the people were saved by the help of the good White Witch of Amboto!

Words in Euskara:

alkatea: mayor, alcalde in Spanish

Anboto: the village called Amboto by the Spanish.

Anbotoko: of Amboto, from Amboto.

eremuan: field

Euskal Herria: the Basque Country where Spain and France touch.

euskal herritarrak: natives of the Basque Country.

Euskara: the Basque language.

gari: wheat.

gari-eremuan: wheat field

gorria: red.

larunbatean: Saturday

Sorgina: witch.

zuri: white (adjective. the noun is zuria.)

On the Atlantic Shore
of North Africa

North Africa in the year 1492 was a colorful mixture of races and nations. People from the heart of Africa had come around the northwest coast of Africa in boats and lived in the large cities along the Atlantic shores in what are now the nations of Senegal, Mauritania, Western Sahara and Morocco. People from the Middle East had migrated across the northern coast of Africa (which is the southern shores of the Mediterranean Sea) and settled in Morocco, which also has an Atlantic coastline. People from Spain and Portugal had come across the Mediterranean Sea to the cities of Melilla and Ceuta. Everyone brought their traditional stories with them, and told them in the early morning hours of October 13, 1492.

Gold Coast African Stories

After the fall of the ancient Empire of the Ghana (the empire was called Wagadougou [Wah-gah-DOO-goo], its leader was called The Ghana) in the year 1217 , the Ashanti People traded gold along the Volta and White Volta rivers flowing south across Africa to the Atlantic shore. The Ashanti took with them their stories of Anansi, the Spider Trickster. Anansi is the word for spider in the Akan language. Just as gold from Africa traveled south to the Gold Coast (from Cape Three Points to the mouth of the Volta), then west and north to Morocco and

Europe, so stories of Anansi went south, then west, then and north as far as Morocco with traders and warriors.

On the creaking deck of a gold-trading ship, gliding all night up the Atlantic shore toward Morocco, men and boys of different tribal origins and different religions drank coconut water and told stories. One man from the Ashanti People told stories about Anansi the Spider.

Why Anansi Has a Narrow Waist

Anansi the Spider is sweet-mouthed. That means he's always hungry, always greedy for something good to eat. And yet, his waist is so narrow! How is that possible? Here's what happened.

Anansi had a big fat waist like a pig in the early days long ago. One day Anansi was walking along a path in the forest about mid-day and he came to a little village. The people saw him coming and said, "Come, Anansi, come! Come join us for lunch. Our pot is almost boiling. Food will be ready soon!"

Anansi thanked the people, but he said, "I'm a very busy creature. I've got important things to do." He spun a long thread from his web spinner and gave the end to the chieftain of the village. "Hold this thread, and when food is ready, give a tug. I'll come and join you for lunch!"

The chieftain agreed and Anansi tied the other end of the thread around his waist and walked on. The path turned west and Anansi came to another village. Everyone knew Anansi, so they said,

"Come, Anansi, come! Eat with us. The meat is almost cooked over the fire!"

"I'm a very busy creature. I've got important things to do." He spun another thread. "Pull on this when the meat's ready, and I'll come and join you." He tied the second thread around his waist and walked on. The path turned south and Anansi came to another village. The same thing happened in six villages.

Anansi, he's so greedy, he sat in a clearing near all six villages, waiting for the food to be ready! He was so hungry he couldn't stand it, but he had six big meals coming! Suddenly one village pulled their thread tugging Anansi in their direction. Far away, they called "Come, Anansi, come! Stew is ready!"

Anansi jumped up and started in the direction of the tugging thread, but another village tugged, yanking him backward. "Come, Anansi, come!" they called far away. "Meat is cooked!"

Anansi turned and started toward the second village, when two other villages tugged on their threads!

Soon all six villages were tugging on Anansi at the same time calling, "Come, Anansi! Come!" The threads pulled him this way and that! The threads got tighter than tight! The threads squished him and squashed him until his fat waist was very, very narrow. He got no lunch that day, and his waist has been squashed down skinny ever since.

Greedy Anansi!

Why Anansi has a Bald Head

Greedy Anansi is always hungry. He's sweet-mouthed. He never wants to share his food with anyone. His head is bald today, but in the long ago days he had a full head of hair. This is what happened.

One day Anansi was sitting in front of his house cooking beans in a iron pot over a hot fire. He put in onion, garlic, salt, olive oil, and hot pepper oil…called mako in the Akan language…to season the beans. He cooked them hot, hot in the iron pot. Just then three of his friends came walking along the forest path: Dog, Guinea Fowl and Rabbit.

Now, greedy Anansi, he did not want to share his beans with anyone, so quickly he dumped the hot, hot beans into his hat and threw the iron pot into a bush. As his three friends walked up, he put his hat full of hot, hot beans on his hairy, hairy head.

"Hello, Anansi," said each of the friends.

"Hello!" said Anansi, with the hot, hot beans soaking into his hair. "Too bad you can't stay!"

The three friends sat down. "Oh, we have plenty of time," said Dog. "We'll stay for a nice visit."

"Ow!" said Anansi. "I mean…Oh!...how nice." The hot beans soaked through his hair and hit his head.

"Warm today," said Miss Guinea Fowl in her high voice, "isn't it?"

"Hot!" said Anansi. "Hot-hot-hot!" He began to jump around in pain. The hot, hot beans were burning his head! "Hotter than hot!"

"Nice blue sky, though," added Rabbit, chewing on a leaf of grass.

"Blue! Blue! Hotter than blue blazes!" said Anansi, hopping in a circle, the beans burning his head..

"What's wrong, Anansi?" asked Dog, casually.

"Wrong? Nothing's wrong!" said Anansi in terrible pain. "But today, in my home village, it is a holiday and I've got to go!" Anansi was starting to shake his head and make his hat full of hot beans wiggle, hoping to ease the pain. "I've got to go dance!"

"What dance are they doing in your home village?" asked Rabbit, politely.

"It's the hat-shaking dance!" Anansi said, jumping around in pain. "And I'm anxious to go join my People!"

"We'll go with you," said Miss Guinea Fowl. "Sounds like fun!"

Anansi was now leaping in the air, whirling around, hopping on one foot then another then another…he has eight, remember.

"No! No!" squealed Anansi as the beans burned his head completely bald. "It's a very secret dance, you shouldn't even be watching me now! Ow! Now! Ow! Now!"

Anansi ran into the forest on his six unoccupied legs, still holding his hat on his aching bald head with the other two.

"Good-bye! Yiiie! Yiiiie! Good Byiiiiie!" Anansi ran away screeching in pain, ran out of sight and jumped in a river, bald as a gourd.

"Funny dance he was doing," said Rabbit.

"Not a very happy dance, either,' said Miss Guinea Fowl.

"Yeah," said Dog. "And every time he wiggled his hat, I thought I smelled beans."

Greedy Anansi.

Moroccan Middle Eastern Funny Stories

People from as far away as Arabia came along the North African coast, settling from Egypt to Morocco, in the 700's and 800's by the modern calendar. They brought their languages, their religions and their traditional stories. Camel drivers and pack-mule drivers were always the subject of funny stories. Here are the best ones they told about a rather simple muleteer...who led caravans of mules from town to town... named Joha.

Joha Bids on a Mule

Joha is dreaming. Joha dreams he is at the souk (marketplace) trying to buy a new mule. He dreams that he and the owner are haggling over the price.

"I'll give you 10 silver coins for him!" says Joha.

"I must have 13 dirhams!" answers the seller, using the name of the local silver coin.

"Eleven!" says Joha.

"Thirteen!"

"Eleven," says Joha. "Take Eleven, you fool! If I wake up, you get nothing!"

Joha's Neighbor Asks a Favor

Joha's lazy neighbor comes over and asks to borrow Joha's little pulling mule to plow some land for a garden.

Joha doesn't want to loan the jack to the lazy man, who is always borrowing things.

"I sold him," says Joha, starting to close the door. "Sorry!"

Just then the jack brays in the back yard and the lazy neighbor hears it.

"You didn't sell him," says the neighbor. "I heard him bray just then!"

"Who are you going to believe?" demands Joha, insulted. "Me? Or some jack ass?"

Joha's Mule Wanders Off

Joha's other neighbor comes to the door another day. Joha is not very bright.

"Joha," the good neighbor says, "your little mule wandered off and I found him lost in the woods!"

"Thank Heaven I wasn't riding him!" says Joha. "I would have been lost, too!"

Joha's Son Drives a Nail

Joha and his son are repairing the wooden walls of the mule shed. Joha's son is not very bright. The boy is holding the nail backwards, with the head against the board, and hitting the point with the hammer.

Joha laughs. "Foolish boy," he says, shaking his head wisely. "Can't you see that the nail you are holding…belongs in the opposite wall behind you?"

Joha and the Bucket Wheel

Joha can be clever sometimes. Joha is sitting on a stool in the shade of a tree drinking honey-water. A few steps away, Joha's best mule is walking in a circle, turning a horizontal wheel which is geared and turns a vertical wheel with buckets mounted on it. The upright wheel dips each bucket into the wadi (stream) and then turns the bucket of water over so that it empties into a wooden trough that leads to the garden.

The mule walks in a circle for an hour and the garden is completely watered for the long, hot day.

Joha's neighbor comes along and finds Joha starting to doze off.

"JOHA," says the neighbor, loudly.

Joha jumps and sits up.

"Joha," asks the neighbor, "how do you know the mule won't just stop working when you doze off?"

"Ah," replies Joha. "The mule wears a little bell on a string around his neck. When he walks the bell jingles. If the little bell stops jingling, I know he's quit working."

"What if," asks the neighbor, "the mule stops working and just rocks his head to jingle the bell and make you think he's working?"

"When the mule gets that smart," said Joha, "he will sit in the shade drinking honey-water and I will turn the wheel!"

Joha and the Jack

Joha the Muleteer is going to the souk in a nearby village. He has a young jack (a donkey colt) who is old enough to sell to a good driver who will treat the colt well. Joha's son comes along. It is only about 5 ghalvas [about half a mile] to the souk, and Joha walks leading the jack. The closer Joha gets to the souk, the more people he passes.

One young man wearing a turban stops Joha and says, "You should make use of the donkey! You are old and full of years. You should ride." Joha agrees and climbs on the sturdy little animal. His son walks alongside.

They go a few orgyes [twenty paces] and a woman wearing a veil scolds Joha.

"You are a grown man! You should let the little boy ride! His legs are shorter and he must trot to keep up!" Joha agrees and trades places with his son.

As Joha get a few more orgyes closer to the market he meets a group of old men who complain to him. "Look how the little jack sweats. You should not even put a boy on him in this heat. Take the boy down!" Joha agrees and takes his son off.

When they arrive at the souk, everyone stares at Joha.

To shut everyone up, Joha is carrying the donkey colt across his shoulders and his son is walking behind him.

Joha and the Joint of Meat

Joha the Muleteer hired a servant. The servant cooked and swept the little clay-brick house with its red tile roof. One day Joha went to the souk and saw a joint of meat [a leg bone with meat like a turkey leg] that looked good. It was already cooked with spices. He asked the butcher to weigh it on his large, hanging balance scale. The meat weighed three librae [the old Roman pound.]

Joha purchased the meat and brought it home. He laid the joint of meat on the table to be eaten after he washed up. When he came back into the kitchen, the meat was gone!

Joha called his servant.

"Where is the joint of meat I laid upon the table?" he demanded.

"I am so sorry, sayyid," said the servant, using the polite word for master. "Your cat came in and ate it."

"Bone and all?" demanded Joha.

"She buried the bone in the back yard," said the servant.

Something about that did not seem right to Joha, but, being a trusting soul, he grabbed his steelyard, a kind of balancing weight used in his caravan business, and set it upon the table. He called his cat, which came to him and meowed. He lifted the cat onto the steelyard and balanced the cat with three weights of one libra each.

"The meat weighed three librae!" Joha declared. "The cat weighs three librae!"

He turned to the servant.

"If this is the cat, where is the meat? If this is the meat, where is the cat!"

The servant ran away and was never seen again. Joha, his son, and the cat ate mush for supper.

Moroccan Jewish Stories

Morocco has always been a nation where Jews, Muslims, Christians and animists have lived together, sometimes openly, sometimes under oppression. At one time, the King of Morocco collected a special tax from non-Muslims. In 1492, there was a large Jewish population in two coastal cities of Morocco, named Ceuta and Melilla. Many Jews had come from Spain, and brought with them stories of their ethnic group.

The story behind the next story: During the Middle Ages (roughly the years 1066-1492) some Jewish mystics in Europe and North Africa carefully read the Sefer Yetzirah (Book of Creation) looking for the mystical ability to create out of unformed matter (for example, a lump of clay) called golem in Hebrew, a living being who would be their servant. The Book of Creation doesn't really say anything about a golem directly, but they were hoping! These mystics believed that a golem…a statue made of clay in the likeness of a man…could be brought to life by scratching on its forehead the Hebrew word for truth (*emet*.) When the golem's work was done – saving a Jewish community in danger, for example – the rabbi (Jewish priest) who made the golem would rub out the first letter of emet on the golem's forehead, leaving *met*, the word for dead. The golem would return to clay. Other legends say the golem was activated and deactivated by a piece of parchment paper with something written on it placed in the golem's mouth or ear. Apparently, in Ceuta, it was placed in the golem's ear.

A gold merchant's family in Morocco were up before dawn, and after morning prayers the grandfather entertained his grandchildren with this story. There is a park in Ceuta next to a medieval castle. It has many statues. Most are beautiful. One is ugly. This is the story about how the ugly statue got there.

The Golem City of Ceuta

There was an old rabbi in the city of Ceuta (THEH-oo-tah) on the coast of Morocco just where the Atlantic Ocean mixes with the Mediterranean Sea. He had studied the ancient Book of Creation and knew many secret things. He was the oldest rabbi in the city, and he lived alone in a large, two-story home. His house was always spotlessly clean, even though his wife had passed away years before, and his gardens were planted with perfect rows and grew abundant vegetables. The rabbi was always out in the community helping people, and no one knew how he could possibly have time to do all the work around his well-maintained house.

One week the oldest rabbi had to go to another city on religious business, and he invited a very young and inexperienced rabbi to house sit for him. He only gave one instruction to the young man. He said, simply, "Don't go into the basement." And he departed.

As soon as the old man was out of sight, the young and rather foolish rabbi ran down to the basement. There he saw an amazing thing! It looked like a stone statue of a very tall, muscular and extremely ugly man. Its eyes were smooth stone, its nostrils and mouth were solid stone and one ear was solid stone. Oddly enough, the statue's left hear had a hole drilled into it, just like a person's ear.

The young man stood up on tiptoes and looked at the ear hole. Lying on the shoulder of the statue, just below the ear hole, was a rolled-up piece of paper exactly the right size to go into the ear. Foolishly, the young man slid the paper into the statue's ear, just to see what would happen.

Making an awful creaking sound, the statue's head turned and looked at the young man with solid stone eyes.

"Give me something to DO!" commanded the stone being. "I am the Golem of Ceuta! I do all my Master's heavy work!"

The thing grabbed the young man and lifted him high in the air as if the man weighed no more than a cup of tea.

"Give me something to DO!"

"Mop the floor, wash the dishes, hoe the garden and sweep the basement!" said the young man in desperation. The golem dropped him and went to work.

The young rabbi began tossing things about in the oldest rabbi's study room, looking for anything that would help him control this huge and powerful stone being. The stone monster thundered into the study and picked the young man up, shaking him.

"Give me something to DO!"

"Wash the windows, straighten the study room, paint the window sills and plant fifty rows of cabbage!" the young man screamed in fear.

The golem stomped away and the young man ran to the old rabbi's bedroom and tore the place apart looking for the Book of Creation or anything that would help him control the monster.

Only a moment later the thing reappeared, all its chores completed, and grabbed the young man shaking him even harder.

"That was too EASY!" shouted the golem. "Give me something to DO!"

"Cut the grass, trim the hedges, prune the fruit trees, and do the laundry!" the young man squealed. The golem dropped him and went to work.

The young man ran to the house of the second-oldest rabbi in Ceuta. Before he could catch his breath and explain what foolish thing he had done, the golem smashed down the second-oldest rabbi's front door and grabbed the young fool. The golem shook him like a rag doll.

"That was TOO EASY!" roared the monster. "Give me something to DO!"

The second-oldest rabbi said softly, "Golem!"

The stone creature stood perfectly still and turned slowly toward the second-oldest rabbi.

"Yes…Rabbi?" it said, quietly and politely.

"I have eight grandchildren. They are all in the park by the castle with the fountain and the statues. They play there every day but the Sabbath. Go to the children and…"

He said the next part very slowly and clearly: "…answer all their questions."

"Yes…Rabbi," said the thing quietly and politely. It dropped the young rabbi in a heap on the floor and stood the door back up behind it as it left.

Down in the park the huge thing sat down and called the children to it.

"I will answer all your questions," it said.

"Why is the sky blue?" one boy asked. "Why doesn't it ever

rain up?" asked a girl. "Why do cats and dogs not like each other? Who invented spanking? What color is the inside of my nose? Are pickles happy? Where did the worm leave his legs? Orange is a color...is banana a color? What makes dirt dirty? Can birds fly back wards? Who combs your stone hair? Do dogs ever burp? Are geese as loud when they're at home? Why do elephants have long noses? Where did I leave my dolly? Are rain drops round or tear shaped? Did you ever see a duck who could dance? Can we eat some mud? Will you tie my shoe? What's another word for synonym? Is it dark inside an egg? What's the stuff between my toes?

Slowly the Golem of Ceuta reached up to its left ear...

...slowly it pulled out the piece of paper...

...slowly it turned back into stone.

And it's still there today, by the fountain, content to do absolutely nothing, like all the other statues.

The Magical Pomegranate

In the city of Fez (FEHZ), just up the Sebou (SEH-boo) River Valley from the Atlantic Ocean, there lived a poor man named Menachem. He could find no work, and had no money. His wife, who had been a seamstress, and made good money sewing for the rich people, had died. He sometimes had to beg for food for himself and his two children.

One day Menachem was in the market and saw a merchant's stall, covered by a canvas awning, where a fruit vendor was selling grapes…a local product…to a rich woman. While the vendor was not looking, hungry Menachem sinned by stealing a beautiful, sweet, ripe pomegranate off the wooden table of the vendor. Pomegranates were rare in Fez, and very expensive.

He thought he would take the pomegranate to his children, but he was so hungry he peeled the fruit open and gobbled some of its seeds and sweet pith. Suddenly someone tapped him on the back. He looked over his shoulder.

Standing there was a fierce-looking soldier of the Sultan's Guards, wearing a tunic, armor, a cape, and an iron helmet. He held a spear in his hand.

"Where did you get that pomegranate?" the soldier asked sternly.

Menachem, who often made up tales to amuse his children, quickly began to make up a tale.

"You can't take this magical pomegranate to the Sultan! I found it! Only I can take it to the Sultan!"

The soldier looked puzzled.

"Well," said Menachem, "He probably would reward you, too, for getting me safely to him…but the riches he will give for it are to be mine, not yours! I found the magical pomegranate!" Menachem pointed at the crowd all around him. "These people are witnesses!" he said even louder. People turned at looked. "You can't take my magical pomegranate to the Sultan for a rich reward!"

The soldier squinted his eyes and stared at the poor man. He seemed to be thinking.

"Follow me!" the soldier said, and turned, striding down the dirt street, his cape flowing out behind him. Menachem thought he had better do what the soldier said. He followed the soldier all the way to the Palace of the Sultan. In just a moment he was standing in the Sultan's garden, surrounded by many soldiers.

The Sultan walked slowly out the doorway and into the garden.

"My soldiers tell me you have a magic pomegranate for me," said the Sultan, dressed in a silken robe. He held out his hand.

"Yes, Mighty One," said the poor man. "I know you will give me a chest of silver and gold to reward me for this wonderful fruit! I found this magical pomegranate in a cave inhabited by a djinn."

"A genie?' the Sultan asked, surprised. "What does this genie's magic pomegranate do?"

"When planted in your garden, it will grow overnight into a tall tree with many beautiful fruits for the Mighty One's table. But there is one problem, Mighty One. The pomegranate seeds must only be planted by a person who is pure of heart…an honest man who has never done anything wrong!"

"What happens if the seeds are planted by someone who has done wrong?" asked the Sultan, curiously.

"Why…the seeds would just lie there under the dirt and not grow in a single day! Then Your Mightiness would be very displeased! But do not worry, My Sultan. Let your trusted and worthy Captain of the Guards plant it for you!"

The Captain spoke quickly. "I cannot plant it…Mighty One! It would not grow and you would know I have done wrong. I once took a reward that should have gone to a younger soldier in my command! Let your most honest and wisest adviser, your Vizier, plant it!"

The poor man held the pomegranate out to the Sultan's wise man, called a vizier. The wise man stepped back a step.

"Mighty…One…" said the Vizier. He seemed to be thinking. "I cannot…plant the seeds. I confess I once stole an idea from another wise man and told you it was my idea. The…the seeds will not grow if I plant them. Let the Royal Treasurer plant the seeds. You trust him with all your wealth. Plant the seeds, Royal

Treasurer, so the Mighty Sultan can have pomegranates at breakfast tomorrow!"

Menachem turned to the Royal Treasurer, offering him the pomegranate.

Now the Royal Treasurer stammered and said, "I…not I… Mighty One…I must admit that I once kept for myself part of a payment made in Your Name, Mighty One!"

The poor man turned to the Sultan. He held out the wet cluster of seeds.

"Surely, Mighty One, you are the only honest man here. You shall plant the seeds, and when they grow into a fruiting tree by sunrise you shall have fresh pomegranates on your table!"

Menachem laid the broken-open pomegranate in the Sultan's hand and bowed, then stepped back. The Sultan slowly turned red in the face.

"I cannot plant the seeds," said the Mighty One. "As a boy I stole a silver dagger from my father and have hid it to this very day." Slowly the Sultan smiled at Menachem. "You were bringing this amazing gift to me…instead of keeping it for yourself. You must be very honest! Surely you must be the one to plant the seeds!"

Menachem shrugged. "I cannot, Mighty One. I'm a thief. I stole this pomegranate from a stall in the market because I was poor and hungry. It isn't even magical. I'm sorry."

Slowly everyone turned and looked at the Sultan to see what horrible punishment he would pronounce for the poor man.

Suddenly the Sultan burst out laughing!

"This humble man teaches us a lesson we all badly needed to learn!" shouted the Sultan. To Menachem he said, "You shall never go hungry again, My Friend!" To his Royal Treasurer he commanded, "Give him a chest of silver and gold and send him on his way! And take not a coin of it for yourself!"

The Sultan turned and walked into the palace, still laughing, eating the rest of the pomegranate.

Menachem went home on a camel of the Sultan's, guarded by four soldiers on foot, leading a donkey with a wooden chest of silver and gold.

And the Royal Treasurer did not keep a single coin for himself!

Afterword for Parents, Teachers, and Librarians

As of the year 2012, Richard Alan Young and Judy Dockrey Young are professional storytellers with sixty-seven years of storytelling experience between them. Judy has been the Storyteller at Silver Dollar City for 35 seasons. The couple have published nine books of storytelling and stories through August House (see www.AugustHouse.com) and five are still in print as ink-and-paper books (Most paperbacks only stay in print five years or fewer. Favorite Scary Stories of American Children, their best-selling book, has been in print for 22 years!) Some of the Young's books are now available for e-readers at www.amazon.com. The Youngs have traveled across the United States and Mexico, and Richard has been to sixteen other foreign countries, always collecting stories. They have performed at festivals, schools, libraries, theme parks, and universities in Arkansas, Colorado, Florida, Iowa, Kansas, Louisiana, Michigan, Nebraska, New Mexico, Oklahoma, South Dakota, Tennessee, Texas, Utah, and Wyoming.

As the Silver Dollar City Storyteller, 1979-2012, Judy has performed over 15,000 shows for a collective audience of about 1,000,000 listeners, (re-counting many who have come to see her shows several times over the three decades.) She plans to be back next year! Richard and Judy selected the stories for this collection based on tell-ability, family values in the stories, authenticity (even silly fiction must not sound fake!), the use of the strengths of the oral medium over the written medium (they are written down as we tell them, not written as if they were short stories), and cultural accuracy. The Youngs have told aloud to an audience every one of the stories in this collection many times. These tales are tried and true.

TEACHERS AND LIBRARIANS: Here are salient points for teaching or leading discussion on some of the stories, listed by name in the order they appear in the book.

On Board the *Pinta*: Don Juan Calderón Mata Siete: See Sources. Compare and contrast this Spanish version with English and German versions, called The Little Tailor (and some other short phrase.)

On Guanahaní: Cave of the Face Paint: See Sources. Compare and contrast this myth with similar European world origin myths of the Norse, Greeks, Romans, etc.

On Board the *Niña*: The Cat Who Became a Monk, The Example of the Pig and the Mule, House Mouse and Country Mouse, Lady Owl's Child, The Lion and the Rabbit: These five exemplos (examples, fables) make a good comparison with those of Aesop and Chaucer, as well as the work of modern fabulists.

In Zempoala: The Totonac, The Legend of Xanath: Myths are often used to explain the origin of natural things and human behavior. Compare this to the Greek myths of Narcissus or Hyacinthus, for example.

The Otomí: Old Dog and Young Coyote, The Aztec Letter, Little Rabbit and Coyote: Otomí stories are technically folktales, the myths and legends of their ancestors are lost, replaced by the myths of the Aztecs who conquered the Otomí. Folk stories of American Indian/African-American Br'er Rabbit and the French tales of Renard and Chanticleer are good comparisons or parallels. The three stories presented have had one small change made to set them in 1492. The rabbit in the third tale was a lamb in the modern version; but sheep were unknown in the Mezquital until the 1530's.

Aztec Overlords of Zempoala: Smoking Mountain: This is the best-known Mexican legend, and is told in dozens of versions depending on who is telling it and where in Central Mexico they live. This is Richard's telling, learned in Mexico in June of 1971. It contrasts well with Romeo and Juliet and other star-crossed lover stories.

Hungry Coyote's Lament: This poem is a slightly abbreviated new English version of a deeply philosophical song written and performed by the King of Texcoco, Netzahualcóyotl. (The poem would bog down in Aztec words, causing disinterest in the reader, if it were not abbreviated.) See the Sources section for more information. The original meter in the Nahuatl language is unknown to these collectors. The 1845 Spanish translation is presented in stanzas of six short lines, with three beats per line. This structure has been preserved as much as is practical in Richard's new translation.

Wailing Woman: This scary story is the most common folktale among Hispanics from Mexico, Central America, and the American Southwest. It is usually called La LLorona (The Wailing Woman) and exists in dozens of variants. Richard learned this in Mexico during a month-long tour with college friends Hank and Becky Hartman in June of 1971.

Skeleton Man: This story has two variants; one occurs between a gambler and a priest and is set in the 1600's. This earlier reconstructed variant is based on the recent discovery (in the

1970's) that some Nahua people still play patolli, even though it was outlawed by Spanish priests in the 1500's. The revelation about patolli occurred as small Indian villages finally brought our their five-hundred-year-old huehuetli, or sacred drums, that they had kept in hiding since they were also outlawed in the 1500's!

In the Ruins of Tajín: The Dance of the Birds: It is important for non-Indians to understand that when North-, Central-, and South-American Indians dance, they are almost always praying. Only a very few social dances exist, where men and women dance together for pleasure and romantic encounters, to prepare the dance grounds, or to re-enact historic events. For example, Plains tribes have a grass-flattening dance that is designed to make a good stomp ground for their dances.

On Board the *Santa María*: The Poem of El Cid: English rhyme is based on a similarity of several sounds at the end of a line, usually one stressed vowel and two or more consonants. Catch rhymes with thatch, fool rhymes with pool, sprocket rhymes with pocket, etc. In medieval Spanish poetry (and in most modern Spanish poetry today) two words rhyme if they have the same stressed last vowel. *Sabor* rhymes with *onda* [o-o], *viento* rhymes with *mientras* [e-e], *hacha* rhymes with *pasará* [a-a], etc. To native English speakers, this doesn't sound like rhyming at all…but to Spanish speakers it does! It is usually called assonant rhyme is English. Even more odd (to English speakers), more than half of the 3,730 lines of El Cid have the same rhyme! That would be impossible in English! Each line of the epic consists of three beats followed by a caesura (a break in writing and a very short pause in speaking) then three more beats. The last beat in the majority of lines is a word with a stressed a in the last syllable [for example adobar, which is not in a rhyming position in the example below] or a stressed a in the next-to-last syllable, and an unstressed o in the last syllable [palacio]. Here is a sample:

Penssaron de adobar essora el pal<u>a</u>cio,
por el suelo e suso tan bien encortin<u>a</u>do,
tanta pórpola e tanto xámed e tanto paño preci<u>a</u>do.

Those are lines 2205-2207, the first three lines spoken by the cabin boy, shown in their original medieval Spanish spelling and grammar. That pattern exists in the majority of the 3,730 lines! If you want to find the recited portions in a copy of the original epic poem, the portion of the Poem of El Cid recited by the night watchman is the First Cantar, the section traditionally marked 1, lines 1-77. The portion of the Poem of El Cid recited by the cabin boy is the Second Cantar, the section traditionally marked 111, lines 2205-2277.

On the Central American Mainland: The Dwarf of Uxmal: Stories like this one have many purposes: explain the origin of a plant and an insect, give a moral lesson on love and courage, teach a pattern of folk belief (magic, the use of rattles in magic), teach tolerance for differently enabled persons, amuse children (who are assistants to the hero), and teach cultural history. Stories told by American Indians are almost always multi-layered in purpose (i.e. not merely to entertain.)

On the Atlantic Coast of Florida: The Mocama Band of the Timucua, The One-Legged Beings: All plant-and-animal-origin stories told by American Indians teach one lesson above all: respect for the earth and renewable/replenishing relationships with plants and animals.

On the South American Mainland: Tamosi and the Tree of Life: Most Central- and South-American Indians have a story of a tree at the center of the world or a tree of life at the beginning of the world. Some Maya People, for example, believed there was a tree of life below the earth in a cave in the beginning of time. Tamosi and the Big Canoe: Most South American forest and jungle tribes have a universal flood story. Among the Waorani of Ecuador, the story says one couple dug out the log canoe and sealed themselves in with sap and the animals survived on their own. The Shuar of Peru and Ecuador say two brothers fighting a great snake caused the flood. Concerning the gourd ladles, Columbus himself, in his diary, mentioned that the Carib people carried gourd ladles to bail out their canoes (entry for Saturday, October 13, 1492.) Students should be given examples of native people who were named based on what an enemy called them (When Europeans first asked some tribe "Who are those other people over there?")[For example: The Waorani of Ecuador were called "Auca" for decades, the word for "savage" in the neighboring Quechua language. The Dineh were called "Navaho" (Navajo) for decades, a word in the neighboring Tewa language that means "out in the fields." The Shuar of Ecuador and Peru were called Jívaro for decades, a word from another language.] The Carib were named by an odd process, which some modern linguists explain thus: the Kalinago People had a word caribna which meant "person," but was also associated with taking trophies in war and (possibly) eating the trophies. There is no conclusive archaeological proof, e.g. human bones from a feast, as fancifully pictured in many old movies. Throughout history, after a battle, the winners sometimes took trophies from the dead enemies: Plains Indians took scalps, Vikings took heads, General Custer's men took arms and legs of women and children (that's why the Indians HATED him!) and in

1492 the Caribs sometimes took an arm or leg to hang as a trophy in their home village. (The period of history known as the Middle Ages was a cruel time in all parts of the world!) The Taíno People, who often lost a fight to the Carib, assumed that the Carib ate those arms and legs. (If they did, it was a rare event, and happened only after a war.) Suddenly the word Caribna, as an adjective in Spanish (Caribnal), became canibal or cannibal ("person who eats human flesh.") The word cannibal did not exist before 1492. You can see why the modern Caribs (Kalinago and many other tribal groups) hate the name. Another practice of the Kalinago in the 1400's was to excarnate (deflesh) their elderly dead, slicing the skin off and saving the bones, which they honored in a shrine in their homes as a form of ancestor worship. Anyone seeing a shrine of human bones might jump to the incorrect conclusion that the occupants of the home ate human flesh, which was not at all the case. Although not known to many today, excarnation was also practiced by Christians in times before embalming. Christopher Columbus' bones were excarnated so they could be taken to another place for burial as a skeleton instead of a putrefying and stinking corpse!

On the Canary Islands: Students might benefit from reading Greek myths of Hercules, and Scylla and Charybdis. Seeking images of the Lady of Lluch and the Lady of Montserrat might be of interest.

On the Atlantic Shore of Portugal: See Sources. These are three well-known European folktales or legends. Seek the collections from which they came for comparison and contrast. These are all modern tellings with amusing twists.

On the Atlantic Shore of Spain: The folktales "Black and

Yellow", "Bastianito", and "Witch of Amboto" are found in many Spanish folktale collections. Use the internet or a library to find collections for comparison and contrast. "The Witch of Amboto," as retold here, represents the mixture of ancient beliefs and new Christian beliefs in the Basque Country in the 1400's. Sadly, the folk belief in witches, both good witches and bad witches, led to terrible persecution of Basque people in the 1600's by religious officials who felt that folk belief endangered religious faith. This story was told in secret among Basques for centuries, and has only recently (in the 1800's and 1900's) begun to be told aloud in non-Basque environments. (Exactly the case with many Pre-Columbian American Indian stories!)

On the Mainland of North Africa: Anansi the Spider left Africa and in the 1600's came to America and turned into a lady named Aunt Nancy (with Aunt pronounced like "ont", not like ant.) Aunt Nancy stories are just Anansi stories dressed up differently. Anansi stories are still told in Africa, of course, as well as on the islands of the Caribbean where Africans live, and anywhere in the South that captured Africans or Free Blacks lived.

Joha the Muleteer is a popular folk character, both wise and foolish at the same time, loved by Christians, Muslims and Jews. In Egypt he is called Goha, in Morocco Joha, among Jewish joke-tellers he is called Juha. Some Joha the Muleteer stories are also told about Turkish Trickster Nasreddin Hodja (also written Nasruddin Hodja.)

Moroccan Jewish folktales have been collected for centuries, and collections or anthologies can be found online or in libraries. These two were selected for their tell-ability and listener appeal. There is, in fact, a park beside a castle in Ceuta, called the Mediterranean

Maritime Park. There are statues in the park. Last time anyone looked, there was no statue of a golem.

The Youngs hope that you enjoy this newly revised and edited collection of stories from the historic night of October 12, 1492, when the Late Middle Ages ended and the Modern Age began.

Sources of the Stories

Introduction: Setting Sail With Christopher ColumbusThe Columbus ship and historical material is gleaned from many sources: The Columbus Diary, as transcribed (before the original diary disappeared from a monastery library) by Bartolomé de Las Casas; from Columbus' letter to Rafael Sánchez, written (after the *Santa María* sank) on board the *Niña*, on the way back to Spain, from the facsimile printed by The W.H. Lowdermilk Co., Chicago, 1893; the letter from Diego Colón (Columbus' son) to Bartolomé de las Casas, in 1519; and the letter from Diego Colón to Ximénez de Cisneros, Cardinal Archbishop of Toledo, Spain, sent from Hispaniola on January 12, 1512. Both of the Colón letters – the five-hundred-year-old originals! - are in the Gilcrease Museum in Tulsa, Oklahoma, where the editors of this collection reverently held them and read them in 1988.

On Board the *Pinta*: Don Juan Calderón Kills Seven: This fairy tale is told all over Europe with many different names and in many versions. In English it's "The Little Tailor," the Brothers Grimm called it "Das tapfere Schneiderlein." When Richard told this story at the Conference on Hispanic Drama at Louisiana State University in 1988, Dr. Rolando Hinojosa-Smith, internationally-famous Hispanic author and creative writing professor at the University of Texas at Austin, said, "Richard, I loved the way you told that story! I could see every scene in my mind as you told it!" It was Dr. Hinojosa-Smith who inspired us to write first the book-on-paper, "Stories from the Days of Christopher Columbus," and now this version. Our variant comes from Spanish (meaning both from Spain and in Spanish) stories Richard heard in Quito, Ecuador in 1954-1955.

On Guanahaní: Cave of the Face Paint: Richard read a version of this story copied by Fray Bartolomé de las Casas in the Library of the National Institute of Anthropology and History in Mexico City in June of 1971. It also appears in *An Account of the Antiquities of the Indians* by Friar Ramón Pané (written in about 1498 on the order of Columbus himself) *A New Edition, with an Introductory Study, Notes & Appendices* by Jose' Juan Arrom, Translated by Susan C. Griswold, Duke University Press, Durham and London, 1999, our source for new research in 2012.

On Board the *Niña*: The Cat Who Became a Monk, The Example of the Pig and the Mule, House Mouse and Country Mouse, Lady Owl's Child: These four stories come from El Libro de los Gatos, a Spanish version of the fables of Odo of Cheriton translated in the 1300's. Odo lived from 1185 – 1246. The Spanish version of his book, in fact, was probably named El Libro de los Cuentos, but in medieval Spanish cuentos was still spelled contos and written (to save space on expensive parchment) as cõtos. [The tilde over the o meant it was followed by an n.] You can see how a copyist's flowery writing might accidentally make the tilde over the o in Cõtos look like the cross mark of a G and the top of an a making the word appear as Gatos. The Lion and the Rabbit: This exemplo (fable) comes from the Arabic book Kalila wa Dimna, written in the year 1210. The fable is now told worldwide with a variety of animals as the central characters. The book itself is named for two of its characters Kalila and Dimna who are fennec foxes. In 1251, King Alfonso the Wise of Castille ordered the Arabic version translated into Spanish, making it the first book of stories and fables ever written in Old Spanish. Richard collected these stories from readings in his History of the Spanish Language classes at the University of Arkansas at Fayetteville in 1967.

On the Mainland of Mexico: In Zempoala, The Totonacs, The Legend of Xanath: Judy and Richard first read this legend on a bottle of Xanath vanilla liqueur in a stall in the market in Papantla, Veracruz, Mexico in 1984. We asked the stall keeper, a Totonac Indian, and he told us the legend in greater detail. There are a dozen different versions told by Nahua (descendants of the Aztecs) and other tribes, but this variant is pure Totonac. The Otomís: Old Dog and Young Coyote, The Aztec Letter, Little Rabbit and Coyote. During the summers of 1969 and 1970, Richard worked as a driver and research assistant for his sister Dr. Gloria Young as she did her M.A./Anthropology field research among the Otomí Indians of the Mezquital Valley in the State of Hidalgo, Mexico. Richard heard these stories told by children in and around the towns of El Cardonal, San Antonio Sabanillas, Orizabita and especially Binghú. Special thanks go to Luis Muthé [the younger] of Binghú and Sebastián Salinas of Orizabita who were 16 and 12 when he met them, and to the entire curso tercero at the school in Binghú who giggled hysterically as he read poorly-pronounced stories to them in Otomí, a language he does not speak but can mimic. Richard regards reading to the 1970 class of third graders in Binghú as one of the high points in his life.

These three stories, retold by Richard, are based on modern variants in the book *Cuentos Otomíes*, I.A.I.M. Patrimonio Indígena del Valle del Mezquital, México [City], México, 1955. Third graders retold the stories to him. The three stories listed above were collected in the early 1950's from Otomís named (in the order of the tales) Severiano Ortiz C., Elfego Escamilla Hernández, and Alfonso Salas Trejo. The Aztec Overlords, Smoking Mountain, Hungry Coyote's Lament, Wailing Woman, Skeleton Man: Richard visited Mexico nineteen times in the years between1948-1995, hearing stories on every trip. These are his favorite Aztec stories, collected by him personally from many different Mexican citizens in and around Mexico City over the half-century. "Hungry Coyote's Lament" is Richard's new (2012) English translation for teens of the modern Spanish version quoted in Appendix II (pages 709-713) in "The Conquest of Mexico" by William Hickling Prescott, published in 1843, reprinted in a Bantam Matrix Edition of 1964. The poem was preserved by Fray Manuel Vega in Mexico City in 1792, and translated from Nahuatl into Spanish with no attribution.

In the Ruins of Tajín: The Dance of the Birds: This Totonac story was collected by Judy and Richard from voladores at the end of their dance in the ruins of El Tajín in 1984. Richard gave the voladores a well-deserved tip.

On Board the *Santa María*: The Exile of El Cid, The Triumph of El Cid: These two segments of the epic Poema de Mio Cid are translated by Richard from the Fifth Edition of the anonymous medieval work as published by Espasa-Calpe, S. A. Madrid, 1946, edited by Ramón Menendez Pidal, with 19th Century English versions consulted. Richard read the three cantares [separate parts] of the epic poem in the original medieval Spanish in History of Spanish Literature in 1965.

On the Central American Mainland The Dwarf of Uxmal: Richard read more than one variant of this legend in Spanish in records of Maya folklore kept by the Library of INAH, the National Institute of Anthropology and History (Instituto Nacional de Antropología e Historia) in Mexico City in June of 1971.

On the Atlantic Coast of Florida: The One-Legged Beings: This story is not probably Timucuan, but many accept it as a very probable candidate. The Spanish mission San Pedro de Mocama was founded in 1587 by Fray Báltazar López on an island in the Atlantic just off the shore of the Spanish province of La Florida, about twenty leagues from Saint Augustine (the island is now in the state of Georgia.) We are grateful to Richard and Wynne Tatman, Timucuan re-enactors, for their guidance in Timucuan research.

On the South American Mainland: The Caribs [Karibs], The Tree of Life, The Big Canoe: Richard was personally acquainted with members of the Wycliffe Bible Translators while in Ecuador in 1954-1955, and Richard and Judy have on numerous occasions visited the library of the Summer Institute of Linguistics formerly in Duncanville, Texas, the town in which Richard's father is buried with his extended family. It is from various ethnographic studies of the Kalinago, Kariña, Karijona, and other Karib tribes, done by SIL that these two stories are gleaned.

On the Canary Islands: The Dark Sea, The Phantom Island The Lady with the Candle, Dragon's Blood, Fortunate Isles: These five brief tales were told to Richard in Spanish by members of the Orquesta Maquinaria from San Cristóbal de la Laguna on the Canary Island of Tenerife, under the direction of Damián Ribero, during their residency in Branson, Missouri, for Silver Dollar City's WorldFest in May of 2000.

On the Atlantic Shores of Europe: In Portugal, The Iron Dancing Shoes, The Tower of Ill Fortune: This story is sometimes given the clumsy title "Tower of Ill Luck," and appears in Consiglieri Pedroso's book *Contos Populares Portugueses* published in Lisbon in 1882. The story is ancient and was certainly told as early as 1492. The Three Citrons of Love : These three well-known folktales from Portugal (which are also told in other European nations, including Spain) may have originally come from India by way of the Moors. The Moors invaded the Iberian Peninsula in 711, bringing to Spain and Portugal the oral and written literature of the Near East and India. See F. H. Coelho, *Contos Populares Portugueses*, Lisboa, 1879. "The Three Citrons of Love" is a folk-variant of Story Number Nine found in Day Five of the Pentameron (Il Pentamerone) compiled by Giambattista Basile and published in Italian in 1636. The story in Basile's book was written by him as a literary fairy tale, based on an earlier legend, presumably this one. There is, of course, a fruit called the blood orange that may have helped inspire this story.

In Spain: Black and Yellow: This is one version of "The Bees," an ancient Spanish how-and-why story; the current title hints at, but does not reveal, the ending. Bastianito: This is the Spanish version of a European folktale known in England as "The Three

Sillies." This and other Spanish stories were first heard in school by Richard in the Colegio Americano de Quito, in Quito, Ecuador, (the most provincial of South American countries) in 1954 and 1955. The Young Lovers of Teruel: The best-known Spanish tragic love story, inspired by an apparently true event that happened in the year 1217 in the city of Teruel in the Kingdom of Aragón. The lovers are identified at their tomb as Isabel de Segura and Juan Martínez de Marcilla, even though most versions of the legend call him Diego. This story was studied in History of Spanish Literature at the University of Arkansas in 1966. Anbotoko Sorgina The Witch of Amboto: A frightening Basque story from Northern Spain. The White Lady is a Protectoress of Euskara (Basque) People. A good friend of ours named Kevin is a Basque, and will not discuss his heritage in public (an excess of caution left over from the days of the dictator Francisco Franco of Spain) but with a wink and a nod he confirmed Richard's retelling of this legend he heard in school in Ecuador. The story appears in Felipe Alfeu's book *Old Tales from Spain* published in 1929, and folktale authorities don't agree on how much Alfeu made up and how much was actually told to him in childhood growing up near Guernica in the Basque region of Spain. (You'll need a very detailed map to find Amboto! The village is located about six miles south of Durango, Spain; Durango is about 20 miles southeast of Bilbao. Guernica is ten miles east of Bilbao.) Our Basque friend Kevin insists that our version of the story is essentially correct (any inaccuracies do not matter to him.) Alfeu names the boy archer; the version Richard heard did not give anyone names, as often happens in folktales and legends. (The version Richard's teacher told in 1955 was probably from the 1929 book.) Student tellers may want to eliminate the Spanish and Basque words and use the English equivalents when retelling the story themselves. The authors of this book do not speak Basque and cannot provide pronunciation guidelines as they have done in the Spanish and American Indian stories.

On the Mainland of North Africa: In Morocco, Ashanti Traders on Atlantic Shores, Why Anansi Has a Narrow Waist, Why Anansi Has a Bald Head: Inspired by the telling of Missourian Bobby Norfolk, Cape Verdean Len Cabral, Oklahoman Tyrone Wilkerson, and Arkansan Mary Furlough, the Youngs have heard these stories many times in many settings. Joha Joke-Stories: Inspired by the telling of Mary Grace Ketner of San Antonio, Texas, these stories come originally from Saudi Arabia and are retold in many, many secondary sources, including *The Turkish Jester; or, The Pleasantries of Cogia Nasr Eddin Effendi*, by George Borrow (Ipswich: W. Webber, 1884.)

Jewish stories told by residents in Ceuta: The Golem of Ceuta: Ceuta and Melilla are two coastal exclaves of Spain on the mainland of North Africa. Formerly the ancient Roman city of Septa, Ceuta was in the hands of the Portuguese in 1492, but had many Jewish residents who had left Spain. A variant of this story was first heard by Richard from an ethnic Jewish family named the Frieds (Freeds) in Quito, Ecuador, in 1955. The Magical Pomegranate: This traditional folktale is widely told in Jewish Quarters of the Old World, and in the United States by immigrants. It is found in many anthologies.

GLOSSARY

An Alphabetical List of Words From the Stories

abide: means to live in.

Acaymo: a mencey or chieftain on the Canary Island of Tenerife in 1392. He received the statue of Our Lady Candelaria, believing it was a statue of Chaxiraxi.

Achbinico: the second cave on Tenerife to which Our Lady Candelaria's statue was taken.

affront: an insult, a rude action.

Akan: the African language of the Ashanti People of the area that includes Ghana.

alkatea: Basque for "mayor."

Amayaúna: the Cave of No Importance, from which all non-Taíno people emerged.

Anansi: the funny spider trickster of the Ashanti People's stories.

Anboto: the Basque name for the village called Amboto by the Spanish.

Anbotoko: Basque for "of Amboto", "from Amboto."

annatto: a tropical plant whose fruit yields a bright red dye and a delicious flavor.

anona: a sweet pulpy tropical fruit with thick scaly rind.

Antón: this man was a native Canary Islander, a Guanche, one of the first to become a Christian.

Aragón: a small kingdom on the northeastern part of the Iberian Peninsula, now part of Spain. King Ferdinand, whose wife sent Columbus to the New World, was King of Aragon (English spelling.)

Ashanti: a great People of East Central Africa in the area of Ghana.

Aztec: a tribe and civilization of Mexican Indians related to the Utes of Colorado and Kansas in the U.S.

Bahamas: the islands north of Cuba, near east Florida, which Columbus called the Lucayas.

bedighted: elegantly dressed

Berber: a People and language of North Africa.

bestow favor: to approve of, and support.

Bobita: "Silly girl" in Spanish.

Branca: "White" in Portuguese; Princess Branca is like Snow White in English.

Bruxa Daninha: Witch Weed in Portuguese.

Bruxa Hamamèlia: Witch Hazel in Portuguese.

buena madrugada: Spanish for "Good Dawning" (after the sun comes up, say "buenos días.")

caballero: Spanish for knight, lord (a royal title), horseman or gentleman.

Caciba-Jagua: a mythical cave from which all Taíno People emerged; Cave of the Face Paint.

cactus candy: a chewy candy made from cactus juice, called *queso de tuna* in Spanish. Tuna in Spanish is not a fish, it's the upside-down-pear-shaped fruit of the prickly pear cactus. The "pear" is boiled and the tiny sharp spines float away, leaving a sweet, sticky pulp.

Cahokia: a Mound Builders ceremonial complex located in modern Collinsville, Illinois, across from St. Louis, Missouri, and very near the Mississippi River. The residents of Cahokia traded with other native people as far north as the Great Lakes and as far south as Florida.

Canary Islands: seven beautiful islands off the coast of Africa, belonging to Spain.

Caonao: "Place of Gold," a region of the Dominican Republic, on the Island of Hispaniola.

Carib: sometimes now spelled Karib, the tribal groups that populated coastal Colombia and Venezuela in northern South America and many islands close to South America. Carib is the name given to them by Columbus. They prefer their own tribal names and do not want to be called Carib today.

Caribbean: the body of water around Cuba and Hispaniola, between the Atlantic and the Gulf of Mexico.

carrack: a sailing ship with a wide beam (ship's width) from the 15th and 16th Centuries. See *Santa María*.

Carthage: a city and empire near the Mediterranean shores of central North Africa destroyed in a war with Rome in the 3rd and 2nd centuries before the birth of Christ.

Castille: also spelled Castile, the English name of Castilla, a region in central Spain, where Queen Isabel (also spelled Isabella and Isabelle) ruled in Columbus' lifetime.

Catalán: the language spoken in northeastern Spain around Barcelona, around Valencia on the east coast of Spain, and on the Spanish Islands in the Mediterranean called Majorca (spelled Mayorca in Spanish), Menorca and Ibiza. Catalán and Spanish are similar, but are not the same language.

Catalonia: also called Cataluña or Gataluña, modern northeastern Spain where both Spanish and Catalán are spoken, around the city of Barcelona.

causeway: a solid dirt-and-stone pathway through shallow water, like a modern wooden pier, only made of earth and carved rock.

cavalcaded: proudly rode on horseback in a long line like a parade.

Ceuta: a city on the coast of Morocco that has belonged to Spain since the 1500's.

Chac Mool: also written Chac-Mool, a type of statue representing a Mexican rain god used in the religions of many peoples, including the Toltec and other post-Classic central Mexican ethnic groups (around A. D. 1200), and among people in post-Classic Maya sites (after about A. D. 1100.)

Charybdis: a Greek mythological monster who lived just below the surface of the sea and created a whirlpool to swallow ships when she opened her giant mouth.

Chaxiraxi: the Sun Mother, a goddess of the pre-Christian Guanche religion on the Canary Islands.

Chichén Itzá: an ancient ruined Maya city located in the modern Municipality of Tinum, in the Mexican state of Yucatán.

Chimisay Beach: a beach on Tenerife where the statue of the Lady Candelaria miraculously washed up. The beach is now an extremely popular resort area for European tourists.

Chinaguaro: the first of two sacred caves (caves then were used like church buildings today) on the island of Tenerife in which the statue of the Lady Candelaria was enshrined (before she was recognized as a Christian icon.)

Cipangu: an old European attempt to say and write the name Nippon, or Japan.

citron: a small green citrus fruit smaller than, and more sour than, a lime.

cloak: a heavy cloth cape for a man or woman, usually decorated with embroidery or gold in medieval times.

Cristóbal Quintero: captain of the *Pinta*.

Cristóbal Colón: Christopher Columbus' name in Spanish.

Cristòfor Colom: Christopher Columbus' name in Catalán, probably his native language.

Danza de los Voladores: the Dance of the Birds, or Dance of the Flying Men.

día de fiesta: Spanish for feast day, holiday.

dirham: an ancient Arabic silver coin.

Don Azagra: the husband of Isabel in the "Young Lovers of Teruel" (Spain's equivalent of the Romeo and Juliette story.)

Don García: father of Diego in the "Young Lovers of Teruel."

doncella: Spanish for young lady, a term used in the 1500's and 1600's.

Donzela Cidra: Portuguese for Citron Maiden.

earplugs: in ancient times, ornaments pushed through holes in the earlobe, the ancestor of modern earrings.

el: Spanish for "the" used with masculine nouns.

érase: "it was…" or " it used to be…" in Spanish.

Érase que era…: "It once was…that there once was…" (This could also be translated: "It once was that there used to be…" or "Once, there used to be…") "Once upon a time…" in Spanish.

eremuan: Basque for field. Gari-eremuan is wheat field.

Euskal Herria: Basque for "the Basque Country" where Spain and France touch.

euskal herritarrak: natives of the Basque Country.

Euskara: the Basque language, said in Basque.

exemplos: examples, Spanish fairytales with a moral message.

Fez: a city in Western Morocco about sixty miles upriver from the Atlantic.

flagship: the lead ship in an armada of ships.

forecastle: the raised area in the front of a sailing ship.

Formoso: Portuguese for handsome, Prince Formosa is the Portuguese way of saying "Prince Charming."

Galicia: extreme northwestern Spain, due north of Portugal, on the Atlantic.

gangplank: a moveable wooden ramp that serves as a walkway onto a ship that is docked.

gari: Basque for wheat.

gari-eremuan: Basque for wheat field.

ghalve: an ancient Arabic unit of distance equal to about 1/10th of a modern mile.

Gibraltar: a huge rock island in the narrow strait where the Atlantic meets the Mediterranean.

Gill: (pronounced with a hard g as in got, not a j as in Jill) Will, William or Bill in Portuguese.

girded steel: a medieval expression that means "buckled on (girded) the belt from which his sword (steel) was suspended."

Gold Coast: the region of coastal central Africa running west to east near the modern nation of Ghana. Gold washed down from the mountains in this region in the streams and rivers.

golem: Hebrew for "mass of unshaped material [clay, mud, etc.]," also, the name given to a creature made of clay or similar unshaped material, and brought to life by magic or divine action. Modern Jews regard this as a fairy tale.

Gomara: a region in modern Morocco from which settlers probably were taken to the Canary Islands, and for which the Island of Gomera is named.

Gomera: the fifth Canary island counting westward, at which Columbus' ships harbored for repairs in August of 1492 before leaving to cross the Atlantic.

gorria: Basque for red.

Guadalquivir: a river in the southernmost part of Spain.

Guajayona: the Proud One in the Taíno legend "Cave of the Face Paint."

Guanahaní: the first island Columbus visited in 1492, now believed to be the small island called Samana Cay (formerly known as Atwood Cay.) The islet (small island) is located in the eastern Bahamas, 22 miles northeast of Acklins Island.

Guanches: the original pre-Christian inhabitants of the Canary Islands.

guinea fowl: a bird like a small chicken.

hatpin: a long, sharp, steel pin pushed through the side of a hat, through a tight bun of braided hair, then out the other side of the hat. The pin through the bun of hair holds the hat on in the wind.

Heaven of the Rain God: a place Aztecs believed drowning victims went to; a happy place, unlike the Land of the Dead, where other dead souls went, which was an unhappy place.

Hercules: Greek mythical hero, world's strongest man (called Hèrcules in Catalán.)

hidalgo: a Spanish word for nobleman.

Huastec: a tribe of people living in the dry region of eastern Mexico called La Huasteca.

Huelva: a town in southern Spain on the Odiel River. Some of Columbus' crewmen came from Huelva.

I-arreka-ru: the scolding, chattering monkey in the story of the Tree of Life.

iguana: a big tropical lizard.

Ixtaccíhuatl: a snow-covered mountain near Mexico City; the "Woman Lying Down."

jagua: a plant with a fruit from which an acidic dye is made and used for temporary tattoos.

jousting: sporting horseback duels between knights in which no blood was supposed to be shed.

Juan de la Cosa: Captain of the *Pinta*.

Kalinago: one of the several Caribbean and South American tribes (also Kariña, Karijona, and others) who don't want to called Carib any more.

King Juba II of Mauretania: prominent African king of Numidia, raised and educated in Rome. He lived 48 B.C. until A. D. 23, and may have been the ruler who sent people from Gomara in Morocco to settle the Canary islands.

la: Spanish for "the" used with feminine nouns.

La Gallega: The "Girl from Galicia," nickname of the ship *Santa María*, which may have been built in a harbor in Galicia.

La Gomera: see Gomera, one of the Canary Islands.

La LLorona: the Wailing Woman of Mexican and Central American legends. The Spanish double L, when capitalized, used to include both l's. Now the spelling Llorona is more common.

Lady of Lluch: patron saint of the Mediterranean island of Majorca (spelled Mayorca in Spanish.) Lluch is also sometimes spelled LLuch.

Lady of Montserrat: patron saint of Catalonia (also spelled Gataluña or Cataluña) the northeastern part of Spain.

larunbatean: Basque for Saturday.

league: a medieval measure of distance; on land a league was about 3 modern miles, at sea a league was about 3 and a half modern miles.

leather-headed: hammers for driving nails have iron or steel heads; hammers for striking engraving tools have heads of wood or tightly-rolled leather for softer and quieter impact.

libra: the ancient Roman measure of weight we call a pound, about the same as a pound today (16 ounces.)

litter: a kind of chair mounted on long poles to be carried by four, six or eight men.

lord: any noble person, or king, or owner of a castle; a mythic male Central America god.

Lucayas: Columbus' name for the islands north of Cuba, near east Florida, now called the Bahamas.

Lucayos: the people of the Lucayas Islands (their own name for themselves. It was rare for a people "discovered" by Europeans to get to keep their own name.)

Lukku-cairi: the Taíno compound word for "island people," the Island Taíno's word for themselves; the word Columbus pronounced Lucayos.

Mácocael: He Who Does Not Blink, the mythical guard at the mouth of the Cave of the Face Paint in the Taíno myth. It may mean He-Who-Has-No-Eyelids. He may have been a lizard, or turned into a lizard by the Sun.

Majorca: (Spelled Mayorca in Spanish) the largest of the Spanish Isles in the Mediterranean.

mako: Akan for pepper. Akan is the language of the People of Ghana and surrounding areas.

mass: the ceremony of worship in the Catholic Church.

Maya: the native people of Southeastern Mexico, Belize, Guatemala, Honduras, and El Salvador.

Melilla: a Spanish city (outside of Spain) on the coast of the Mediterranean on the mainland with Morocco.

mencey: a chieftain of the Guanches, the native people of the Canary Islands. Each island had a dozen or so menceys and autonomous regions ruled by them in 1492.

Mezquital: Spanish for "mesquite grove," the name of a valley north of Mexico City, in the State of Hidalgo, near the city of Ixmiquilpan and home of the Mountain Hñuh (Otomís.)

Mocama: the Eastern Band of the Timucua Indians of Florida in the 1500's and 1600's.

Moguer: a town on the Río Tinto in southern Spain. Some of Columbus' crew came from Moguer.

monastery: a private place where monks live to pray and contemplate the nature of life.

Motecuhzoma: the correct name in Nahuatl of the Emperor Moctezuma (Spanish) or Montezuma (English), the last true Emperor of the Aztecs. The Motecuhzoma praised by Netzahualcóyotl in his poem "Lament" was Motecuzoma the First; Motecuhzoma the Second was the last true Emperor of the Aztecs. After the Spanish murdered Motecuhzoma the Second the Aztecs honored two more of his relatives with the title of Emperor, but neither had the authority or power that Motehcuzoma II once had.

muleteer: one who owns, herds, and drives caravans of mules.

Nahua: the modern Mexican Indian language descended from Nahuatl, the language of the Aztecs spoken in 1492.

Netzahualcóyotl: (also spelled Nezahualcóyotl) King of Texcoco in the mid 1400's, and well-known Aztec poet. He was no longer alive by 1492.

niche: a small opening in a larger object or surface; the Temple of the Niches at El Tajín has 100 niches in each of which a statue of a Totonac god probably once sat.

Niña: one of Columbus' three ships.

obsidian: volcanic glass that, when flakes, cracks into blades with an edge thickness of one molecule; the sharpest thing on earth. Once used, the sharpness quickly diminishes.

orgyre: an ancient Arabic measure of distance; about 7-10 paces or 20 to 25 feet.

Otomí: the Mexican Indian tribe of central and eastern coastal people who call themselves the Hñuh.

overlords: rulers forced onto a city or kingdom by conquerors from another kingdom.

Oyoyotzín: a prince of Tlacopán to whom Netzahualcóyotl dedicated a poem about the nature of life and change.

palfreys: a type of horse (not a separate breed) highly prized for riding in the Middle Ages.

Palos de Moguer: a small town on the Tinto River in southern Spain. There is another town named Palos in Spain, so the suffix "de Moguer" tells which Palos (like, say, Springfield, Missouri, and Springfield , Illinois.) Many of Columbus' sailors came from Palos de Moguer, and it is the port from which Columbus sailed on August 3, 1492.

panecillo: Spanish for "little loaf of bread." Usually the size of a dinner roll in the U. S.

patolli: an Aztec board game involving gambling, outlawed in the 1500's by Christian priests.

Phoenicia (Sidonia): a region on the eastern shore of the Mediterranean, now part of Lebanon and Israel.

pictogram: a way of writing with pictures and symbols instead of letters of an alphabet.

Pillars of Hercules: two towering rocks on either side of the Straits of Messina, between Italy and Sicily; later the name referred to the Straits of Gibraltar.

Pinta: the fastest of Columbus' ships; the ship from which land was sighted on October 12, 1492.

pith: the soft insides of a plant product, edible if it is the inside of a fruit.

pomegranate: The pomegranate (scientific name Punica granatum) is a fruit-bearing leafy shrub or small tree native to the area of modern day Iran and Iraq, but now grown worldwide. The fruit has hundreds of seeds surrounded by sweet edible pulp.

Popocatépetl: volcano east of Mexico City, the "Smoking Mountain."

potion: a mixture of herbs for medicine or magic.

quetzal: a beautiful parrot-like tropical bird with extremely long and beautiful tail feathers.

Quetzalcóatl: the Quetzal-Snake god, a giant snake with a ruff or headdress of quetzal feathers, worshipped by the Aztecs.

rabbi: a Jewish religious leader, corresponding to a Christian priest or Muslim mullah.

Río Odiel: a river in southernmost Spain.

Río Saltés: "Salty River," a wide navigable river that allows boats to harbor safely on the Odiel and Tinto rivers, away from storms, yet giving ships access to the Atlantic.

Rodrigo de Triana: Juan Rodríguez Bermejo (also spelled Vermejo), the man who first sighted land on October 12, 1492. (Columbus claimed to have seen a firelight after sunset the night before, and didn't give Rodrigo a reward for sighting land!)

Saiya: the name of an assistant to the King of Uxmal in "The Dwarf of Uxmal."

Samana Cay (formerly known as Atwood Cay) the islet (small island) is located in the eastern Bahamas, 22 miles northeast of Acklins Island.

San Borondón: the name given to the ghost island seen off Ferro (El Hierro), the westernmost of the Canary Islands.

San Sebastián: capital of the Island of La Gomera.

Santa María: the flagship of Columbus' fleet in 1492. No one knows exactly what she looked like, but she was a carrack, or wide-bodied medieval ship about 70 feet long and 25 feet wide.

sayyid: an honorary Arabic title, like El Cid in Spanish, said to a person of higher rank.

Scylla: the Greek mythical sailor-eating monster with one hundred heads (100 was a popular number of heads for mythical beasts.) She lived on land beside Charybdis (see Charybdis.)

Sebou: the river in northwest Morocco that connects the city of Fez to the Atlantic. No sea-faring ships can come all the way up the Sebou, but cargo and trade goods could travel upriver to Fez on smaller boats.

Sefer Yetzirah: the Book of Creation, or more properly The Book of Formation, written around 200 B.C., a book on language, mathematics, and the (perceived) power of numerology. (Unfortunately, there isn't a chapter on making a golem to do your housework or homework.)

señor: Spanish for Sir, Mr., gentleman, man.

señora: Spanish for Ma'am, Mrs., lady, woman (señorita is Miss, young lady.)

Skeleton Man: Lord of the Aztec Land of the Dead.

Skeleton Woman: Lady of the Aztec Land of the Dead, wife of Skeleton Man.

Sorgina: Basque for witch.

souk: Arabic for open-air market with stalls and awnings set up daily and taken down at night.

sultan: a king, noble, or lord of an Arabic-speaking area. The word meant different things in different places at different times, just as a word like "leader" might.

tablets: life-size man-shaped wooden targets which shatter when hit dead center with a lance by a man on horseback. A rider had to break the tablet to win the contest. Part of the sport called jousting.

Taíno: the people and language of the Bahamas, Cuba and Hispaniola, and parts of Florida in 1492. Enemies of the Carib. The first Americans Columbus met.

Tajín: an ancient ruined city, claimed by the Totonac People as having been built by them and inhabited from about A.D. 600 to 1200. El Tajín is located in low rolling mountains near the modern town of Poza Rica in the Municipality of Papantla, north of Veracruz, Mexico.

Tamosi Kabo-Tano: the Creator in Carib stories.

Tépetl: the prince in "Smoking Mountain," Strong or Strong-Like-A-Mountain.

Tenochtitlán: the Aztec city where the Emperor lived, one of the Three Thronhes (kingdoms) of the Aztecs (now completely surrounded by modern Mexico City.)

Tenerife: the largest Canary island.

Teruel: a city in Aragón (a region of Spain) where the "Young Lovers..." story takes place.

Texcoco: one of the three Aztec kingdoms by the lake in the Valley of Mexico, where Mexico City sits today.

Tezcatlipoca: Smoking Mirror (possibly meaning Comet-With-A-Tail; the bright comet would be the mirror and the trailing smoke would be the tail), an Aztec god who demanded human sacrifice.

Three Thrones: the triple alliance of the Aztec kingdoms of Tenochtitlán, Tlacopán and Texcoco in the late 1400's and ending in A. D. 1519.

tiazinha: "Auntie," a term of respect and endearment in Portuguese.

Tlacopán: one of the Three Thrones (see above.)

token: in the Middle Ages, any small gift.

Totóquil: King of Tlacopán in 1480, father of Oyoyotzín, the prince to whom Netzahualcóyotl dedicated a poem about life and fate.

Totomítl: Aztec for archers, origin of the name Otomí. Aztecs did not use bows and arrows, Otomís did.

Totonac: a Mexican people of east central and gulf-coastal Mexico.

Tutunacutachawin: the ancient language of the Totonac Tribe.

Tutunaku: the name the Totonac People call themselves.

tuxwadá: Otomí for (Spanish) maguey blanco or (English) American Agave (a succulent, not a true cactus, but similar to cactus and to aloe.) It is called "white" for the color of its flowers, which form only once in the plant's lifetime. The sap of the tuxwadá is called agua miel (honey-water in Spanish) and is used to make an alcoholic (and therefore germ-free) beverage called pulque. In a desert where water is rare, the agua miel may be the only drink during drought.

tyranny: cruel oppression by a king, government or outside power.

Tzarahuín: Totonac for linnet (a small song bird), and the name of the hero in "Legend of Xanath."

UNESCO: the United Nations Educational, Scientific, and Cultural Organization which works to protect important cultural icons of all the world's different peoples.

Uxmal: a ruined Maya city in Yucatán, Mexico, which was inhabited as an active city from about A.D. 700 to about 1200 and only as an area of worship thereafter.

Valencia: a city (today), a region of Spain (today), and a kingdom in the Middle Ages. Kingdoms in the Middle Ages were very small; Valencia was a city and a small kingdom of only several miles around the city.

vassal: someone who takes an oath to serve a king or nobleman for his entire life.

vestments: the beautiful garments worn by a church leader to remind us of the glory of God

voladores: any flyers, especially the brave young men who hang upside down from ropes whirling around a pole. The dance is performed by several native Mexican peoples including the Nahua, Huastec, Totonac and coastal Otomí.

wadi: Arabic for creek or stream.

Wailing Woman: legendary female phantom called La LLorona in Spanish.

white agave: a large American, cactus-like and aloe-like, succulent (a kind of plant) with wide blades and a once-in-its-life tall flowering stalk with white flowers.

Xanath: the heroine of the legend of the same name.

Xipe Totec: the Aztec God of Fertility whose name replaced the original names of the traditional fertility gods of people conquered by the Aztecs.

Yahubaba: the man called Old One in the Taíno story "Cave of the Face Paint."

Yaya: one of the names for the Taíno Creator.

Yoloxóchitl: Red Flower, heroine of "Smoking Mountain."

Yucatán: the southeastern-most part of Mexico.

Yucatec Maya: the Maya people of Yucatán (not those of Guatemala, etc.)

Zempoala: ancient Totonac city conquered by the Aztecs in 1480, and the Spanish in 1519, now a ruin near Veracruz, Mexico.

zuri: Basque for white (adjective. the noun is zuria)